To

x

Sue Hampton wrote stories as a child, inspired by her father, Paul, who was a poet. Now a teacher in Hertfordshire, she originally began **Spirit and Fire** as a Story Time read for her class when they were studying the Romans. A lot of research went into getting the historical details right.

Her other two children's novels from Pegasus,
Voice of The Aspen and **Shutdown**, will be available in November 07 and early 08.

She writes adult fiction too.

SPIRIT AND FIRE

SUE HAMPTON

SPIRIT AND FIRE

Nightingale Books

A CIP catalogue record for this title is
available from the British Library.

ISBN: 978 1 90349 158 4

*Nightingale Books is an imprint of
Pegasus Elliot MacKenzie Publishers Ltd.*
www.pegasuspublishers.com

First Published in 2007

**Nightingale Books
Sheraton House Castle Park
Cambridge England**

Printed & Bound in Great Britain

To Phan Thi Kim Phúc, who as a young
Vietnamese girl also ran from the fire of war,
and who now works for peace.

Acknowledgements

I would like to acknowledge the encouragement and inspiration of Michael Morpurgo, and the help of Jenny Hall at the Museum of London, who was kind enough to advise on historical detail.

Chapter One

Mouse

Before, when Aifa lived the old life, no one ever asked her whether she was happy. The question did not cross her mind; nor would she have known how to answer it. Until everything changed, she didn't realise how ordinary the living was, how wondrously small and simple her world had always been. She didn't even see the comfort in the pattern, repeated endlessly, like the seasons, like night after day. And though those days weren't all as peaceful as she could wish, she'd come to accept the occasional fight, learning to turn from the raised voices and the brandished iron – as long, of course, as her own father wasn't involved.

"It's the male way, Aifa," her mother told her. "You don't see female robins strutting and pecking to claim their territory."

They watched just such a noisy male, puffed up and loud, his feathers soft but his small eyes hard with confrontation.

"And you notice it's not the peaceful milk-bearers but the big horned beasts that feel the need to charge."

Aifa knew about bulls. One had tried out its bony weapons on her, long ago when she had tottered close enough to wonder at its towering blackness and steaming breath. Her bruises had healed, but she admired now from a respectful distance. The memory of a moment's hurling flight and heavy landing was still vivid enough to quicken her heartbeat.

It had been explained, when she was very young and easily frightened, that fighting was what men had to do.

"Sometimes I think they carry anger with them everywhere they go," her mother said, "ready to use it, like a knife."

She said it without blame, her sigh turning into a fond smile. Aifa knew she was thinking of her father, who was a powerful man, and not just in the breadth of his shoulders and the muscles balling and ridging under his tough brown skin. Being the younger brother of the king meant that others fell silent when he spoke, nodded with respect, shrank from disagreeing. He was an important man, as respected as the holiest Druid. Many feared him, and Aifa well understood why. No man in the village had more loyal retainers to attend him, and no man had a finer mount than Ri, his powerful black stallion. Aifa was proud to see him high on horseback, and her favourite kind of work was grooming the huge, gleaming beast, or feeding him from her hand.

Her father and uncle were often together, laughing, arguing like all brothers, and their wrestling seemed more like sport than battle. Sometimes that was just what it was, when feasts were interrupted by the two of them, draining the beer from their drinking horns, raising their fists and leaping to their feet to entertain their audience. Then all around the circle, the food would be forgotten as heads turned to watch. And Aifa herself had watched, often enough, unsure what to feel as the firelight flickered on their faces and winked off the playful glint in their eyes. Her mother said they were like wolf cubs – big, overgrown and hairy, but no real bite.

14

Aifa loved the way her mother made everything seem alright.

She had been a nervous child and learned, slowly, to pretend to be the brave daughter her father demanded. But still, at night, she sometimes felt afraid, when the earth had no peace. What she feared, more than she could explain, was the earth-cracking roar from above that shook her heart inside her, and the biting light that flashed across the walls of the roundhouse.

Then, waking to comfort her, her mother would look up in awe and murmur the name of Taranis, the Thunderer, god of the sky. But, though she held Aifa's hand tightly, it was clear that she herself was not frightened. She simply promised that the goddess Epona would protect them. She'd even taken the precious symbol of the horse from around her own neck and given it to Aifa, to reassure her. The tiny necklace gleamed in moonlight. When Aifa touched it in darkness she could trace its copper body from its head to its hooves. Her mother had worked it in flame, shaped it, kept it shining. And around her neck it made her feel bigger, braver, and safe.

"One day," her mother would often say, "we'll go and see for ourselves."

"Oh, yes, please," Aifa would agree, and imagine…

Because one day, they told each other, they would travel to the east, where a great white horse had long ago been dug out of the hillside. Her mother had never seen it, but heard of its magic. There, she said, they would wonder at each dip and curve of chalk, shaped with the eyes of a high-flying eagle and the mysterious insight that only gods could give. Then, many miles

15

from their own country, they would bow down in worship of her mother's favourite goddess, and it would feel like coming home.

But though she tried to trust Epona, there were times, even now that Aifa was growing out of childhood and beyond such fears, when she lay awake, her fingers tight around the necklace, her heart tight in prayer. For Taranis could sound so angry, up there in the unreachable clouds, that she pictured his cruel eyes, burning through the straw roof of her roundhouse, seeking her out. Aifa would lie stiff on her horse hair mattress, shivering in spite of the fur that covered her, unable to understand how her parents and baby brother could sleep as peacefully as the animals. It was as if the god of the sky had determined to punish her and her alone – but what had she done?

Perhaps, she thought, it was for her fears themselves that she was punished. For failing to be the kind of daughter her father wanted her to be. For being a lamb when he demanded a bear. But in her mother's eyes she was a good girl. And she tried.

Day after day she helped to grind the grain, until the rough brown skin between her palm and her wrist wore red with the rubbing. Hour after hour she sat teasing the wool to be woven on the loom. She stirred the stew at meal times, while the fumes made her eyes water. And, small though she was, she helped to carry the wood that fuelled the blaze beneath the steaming pot. Aifa worked as hard as she could, ignored the splinters and the scratches, and bore the smoke that curled into her eyes with its bitter sting. She even tolerated the stench of the pigs, and the puddled mud and dung that splattered her legs in the rain.

No one in the village, old or young, warlike or watchful, really complained. But even her mother admitted that life could be hard, especially when the snow froze the earth and sealed it solid. Her own heart, she said, was strong. But she fretted over Acco, the bright-eyed baby brother that Aifa loved. Sparrow, she had nicknamed him, because he didn't weigh much more than the birds, though he had no feathers to puff up against the cold. He had been born small and pale, but if his heart was not as strong as his mother's, it seemed it was brave. Aifa prayed it would keep beating warm through winter.

Her father would tell stories of more violent times when hearts were stopped by knives in the darkness. His own father, like his grandfather before him, had been a warrior. Many times she had heard of daring raids on neighbouring tribes, stealing their cows and weapons in the silence of night. She knew her father liked to think he was a warrior too. But since the Romans came to occupy Britannia, times had changed. Not that anyone dared suggest to Aifa's father that they owed the Romans anything at all.

The Silures lived, in any case, to the west, in a land free from Roman interference. But around them the whole island was settling into a busy peace.

So only once or twice in her thirteen years had Aifa seen her father dressed for fighting, and that had been against an older, less organised enemy across the valley. She still remembered the blue woad on his scarred and bearded face, his hair spiked up on the top of his head like one of those strutting cockerels that was always looking for trouble. It had scared her, but he thought her fear was funny.

"Poor little mouse!" he teased her, and performed his battle cry just to see her scrunch up her pale face and cover her ears.

17

He showed her the blood on his sword.

"No boar this time," he'd told her. "It's human blood I've taken, richer than wine. Look. Smell it."

He brandished the blade with its bright red stain, thrusting it under her chin. Then he wiped it clean, and smiled.

"Ready for next time," he said, and the grin faded into a face so hard that she looked away.

But that time had never come, and for that Aifa never ceased to thank Epona. Looking at Sparrow, as he reached out to grab her finger, or laughed throatily at a chicken pecking at a grain of corn, Aifa hoped with all her heart that he would never roar in anger. That he would never stop delighting in birds, leaves and sunlight... to relish blood instead. After all, he was much too beautiful to scar his cheeks with fighting.

Of course Acco was too young yet even to practise aiming the sling. But Aifa, unfortunately, was not. Her target was usually a hard block of stale bread on the end of a post – and her success rate a terrible disappointment to her father. It wasn't only that her arms were thin and weak, and her aim poor. Her memory did not help, of a day when the posts bore instead a gruesome, grey-skinned warning. It was a day that, much as she longed to, she felt sure she could never forget. She had been small, still unsteady on her legs, and playing in the dirt, when she had looked up to see the blood-trickled faces of the dead staring down at her. Her mother covered her eyes, but the picture was already drawn inside her. And even now in her dreams she was still reminded of the severed heads, the wind teasing the hair into a trick of life, but the flesh as cold and congealed as any other bad meat.

Her father saw that Aifa was not like other girls. He thought his only daughter strangely silent, and wondered whether the gods meant her to follow a sacred path. She knew she troubled him.

"What are you thinking?" he would demand from time to time, when he noticed her suddenly, as if he had forgotten she existed.

Or: "She's thinking again! What are you thinking, girl? Tell me!"

At which her mother told him, "Thoughts too deep for you to understand!"

Such playfulness was dangerous, but when he was merry, he would only laugh. Usually her mother judged his mood well enough to tease him. But then she was his favourite wife – and, being the mother of his only surviving children, the one he honoured most.

She was also Aifa's champion, reminding him that his daughter was more than a thinker with a deep and quiet spirit. She was in fact the owner of nimble and skilful fingers that helped her to sew and weave with unusual delicacy. One day, she hoped, she would be allowed to work in gold, and make something as fine as the horse around her neck. She was still too young. But she was deemed old enough already to play her part in the holy festivals. Not long ago she had helped to decorate the sacred yew near the river with ribbons and hammer coins into its trunk, so that it shone in the sun, its branches waving rainbow colours against the sky.

Aifa loved trees, and it would be high in one less holy tree that she would usually be found, should anyone be looking for her. She didn't shirk her duties, but she did like to watch, and be still. If Sparrow saw her, he would reach up helplessly, so desperate to join her that she'd have to shin down to stop him crying. Stopping his tears was something she could always do.

They were a family like many others in the land, proud but hard-working, living thankfully through each bitter winter and deathly disease. Aifa just didn't know any other kind of life, difficult or easy, happy or sad. She never dreamed that her days or nights could be any different – not until her whole world changed.

Chapter Two

Stories

Aifa knew everyone in the village, even if there were men and boys too loud or brash to speak to, and narrow-eyed, fault-finding women whose tongues she would rather not provoke into sharpness. She had friends, but none whose company was easy, because there wasn't another girl of her own age quite like her. She wasn't a gossip who said one thing to a person's face and quite another when that person's back was turned. And she didn't really care how she arranged her hair. But like everyone, young and old, male and female, she smiled with excitement whenever anyone arrived at the village, with news or with something to sell.

There was an Assyrian with a black beard, whose strange-edged voice carried through the settlement when he had trinkets to tempt them. She needed no jewellery when she had Epona to watch over her, but she loved to see the colours of the necklaces from other worlds, and feel cloth smoother and shinier than anything she could ever weave.

But it wasn't the gleaming stones of the Assyrian that interested Aifa most. It was the fish – or rather the fish seller – who always looked out for her in the gathered crowd and gave her a wave and a smile. She smelt him coming, of course, but she forgave him the stench in his hair and grizzled silver beard. And at least, because the village wasn't so many miles from the sea, the fish he brought had not been dead too long.

21

"It's a treat I have for you today, Aifa!" he called, and swung a fat, shimmery one above his head, as if he might let go and send it flying in her direction.

The others laughed when she couldn't help ducking, but he laughed loudest, and wrapped it in cloth for her so that she didn't have to return its stare. Aifa wished that fish, when they died, would close their eyes and round, questioning mouths. They looked so helpless it made her sorry.

"It might stink a little," he admitted, almost every time, "but it doesn't smell bad enough for the Romans. They let their fish rot for weeks – months – and spice it into a sauce to hide the taste of everything!"

"Do you really sell to the Romans?" she had asked him once.

"Of course," he said, and showed her a coin with a man's head on one side – a man with short hair and a long nose.

"The Emperor!" he told them all, and the way he announced the word made it clear that they were to hear it with hushed wonder, or a gasp of awe.

"Tell us a story," she always asked him, because he took his basketloads near and far, and because he knew how to make his travels sound like adventures.

So she loved to listen to his tales of huge leaping dolphins and stars on the sand.

But his best story of all, though it frightened her, was the tale he told of a morning before she was born, when her mother was the same size as she was now, and her hair, he said, just as wild and fair. It was a story not of dolphins but of crowds of huge white sails, of countless wooden ships as powerful and unstoppable as the tide, and polished bronze glinting in sunlight.

He hadn't waited, he said, to meet the Romans face to face, but he had found those who had – lying bleeding on the beach, the sea licking their fatal wounds. And he had heard, from those who had spoken to survivors, about the armour that made them strong as rock, the spears that pierced from afar, and the shields, the enormous, curving shells that protected them from everything the coastal tribes could hurl at them.

"I thought they were not human," he said, "but gods! Thousands of marching, clinking, heartless gods!"

And though he had met many Romans since, exchanged pleasantries and bartered with them like any other customers, he had not forgotten the fleet that kept on coming, wave after wave, or the fear in the eyes of those who had seen the faces half-hidden by the heavy helmets.

Her mother only shook her head when Aifa asked her about the Romans, and how long they would stay.

"Who knows but Epona?" she sighed.

But when Aifa asked her what right they had to be there, so far from their own land, her mother did not hesitate.

"No right at all! None! It's an ill-mannered guest who barges in where he's not been invited."

She had never really answered the question of whether they would some day seek to extend the boundaries of the province of Britannia to include the land of the Silures, and of the Demetae further to the west.

"They say the best way is to give them what they want," she said, "to pay them their taxes if you have to and hope they let you be. They're too busy building their walls, laying roads straight as arrows. They won't bother us if we don't bother them – and even your father has more sense than to do that."

Aifa wasn't so sure, but he didn't seem frightened either. He talked about the Romans now and then, when he was drunk enough to boast that they'd pay with their lives, the lot of them, if they ever dared to cross him.

"And I'd string up every coward who seeks to be their friend!" he'd roar across the evening flames, wiping his droopy moustache. "It makes me sick to my stomach to hear of their mealy-mouthed peacekeeping. Traitors all of them!"

Of course, speeches like that would go down well with other drunken warriors who waved their swords and shouted their hatred of the invaders from over the sea. But by day her father only cared about the thrill of hunting, and the pride he took in working metal through fire. Aifa felt sure that in sober daylight he would have more sense than to provoke a conflict that would, by every account, be impossible to win. She was only too aware that these Romans were not so many miles away, and she had heard much of their cleverness and power. But, though they meant little more to Aifa than the spirits of ancient tales, there were times, silent, brooding times, when her head filled with the chink of armour, marching feet and gnawing fear.

Chapter Three

Attack!

The gods didn't warn them. No one did. The night was still and the pale moon untroubled by wind. Aifa was sleeping a dreamless sleep when she woke to the panic-sharp yelping of the dogs. Stirring, she made out harsh, shapeless words, unfamiliar voices, sounds that carried no meaning. It was as if she had awoken in a terrifying foreign world in which she could shape no sense. And then, as she sat up and saw her mother's face, lit by flickering flame through the doorway, Aifa realised what they meant, these noises that scared her so much more than thunder.

For a moment they stared at each other, too terrified to move. Then her mother scooped her little brother from the mattress where he had slept beside her. One hand reached to stifle fearful cries from his tiny mouth as she carried him, between her hip and chest, his thin legs hanging. With no hand to grab, Aifa followed, close at her heels. They ran, the three of them, out of the hut, and into a crashing, slashing chaos of metal and screams, and a bitter cloud of smoke.

Bodies littered the mud under their feet. Only moments ago they had breathed, run and cried. Now they were no more than obstacles in their way. Yet Aifa knew, as they stumbled over and past them, that one of these nameless mounds in the darkness must be the one they most feared to find. She knew her father would not have abandoned them. Somewhere nearby he must have died trying to protect them, and as the firelight offered glimpses of faces below her feet, she dared not look down.

But he would be found. He must be found. He was a hero, a warrior after all, and they must honour him with the kind of funeral he deserved. But they were helpless. How, without his body, could they ensure the safe passage of his immortal soul?

She hardly knew where she was, barely recognising anything she saw as they tried to weave a way through the mayhem. Yet flames lit up the homes of the girls she sewed with, the warriors her father hunted with, the women who talked with her mother as they knelt to scrub clothes in the stream. The village was ablaze.

There was nowhere to run but through the tangle of iron and blood. She reached for her mother, but both arms were where they had to be, wrapped around Sparrow, unable to soothe the whimpering sobs that throbbed in the small chest. It was hard to stay close, and even harder to hear, through all the turmoil, her mother's voice calling her name again and again.

"Mother!" she cried, and it felt like the last breath she could find.

Her hair torn by the wind, she pulled it from her face, but still she could barely see through the searing brightness, and curtaining smoke filled her throat as it blinded.

"Mother!" she cried. "Acco!"

But they had gone. His cries had faded away into the shouting and the pain. The blackness had torn them away from her.

Aifa stopped running and stood, breathless. For all the crowding noise, she was alone. She pressed herself against the wall of the hay barn, turning all around her, lost and blind. Her heart ached and her breath was painful. But she listened. The horses! The sudden thought held her still and alert, trying, through the clashing din, to hear among all the cries and snorts the voice of Ri, her father's stallion. She pictured him, whinnying and rearing in fear, but brave enough to leap the fence and carry them far from here. Would her mother be thinking the same and, even now, making her way through the madness to find him? Would she reach out an arm any moment, to pull Aifa onto his great black back behind her?

With a hiss and crackle of hunger, new flame tore into the roof above her and the barn began to melt into the inferno around it. Sparks scattering through the smoke around her head, she ran, thinking only of the clean air and silence that must lie somewhere beyond.

As she stumbled over a body, shrouded in a cloak at her feet, the flames illuminated a long moustache and a stubbled black chin. For a moment she thought... But no. The clasp fastening the cloak at his neck, its snake head glimpsed before darkness returned to bury it from view, belonged not to him, but her uncle.

Aifa wished she had liked him more and feared him less. He would never mock her with a "Mouse" squeak again.

One moment Aifa was running. The next she fell to the mud as something hard and heavy caught the side of her head. Rough hands grabbed her around the waist and lifted her into the air, her short legs too sore and stiff to kick more than the feeblest of protests. Her wrists were tied, so tightly that she groaned out

27

loud, by someone unseen behind her, and she was thrown into a huge kind of cart unlike any she had ever seen. There her eyes met others, as wide-eyed with terror as her own. Aifa tumbled down and slumped on straw.

As the wheels rolled on through the darkness, the sky cracked open in a knifeslash of angry light that brought the first tear to her eyes and chilled her flame-warmed body. Shaken and bruised as the cart gathered bumping, lurching speed, Aifa was carried away from her home, her family and the old life that was all she had known.

It was the beginning of her new life, as a slave.

Chapter four

Copy

Hour after hour she lay in the straw, travelling on and on, with no knowledge of where she was or where she was being taken. Bumped. Thrown. Jolted. Again and again, like waves, rushed the memories of the bodies beneath her feet, and the image of her father's face, smeared with blood, almost too real to be imagined. And if he did lie there in the mud, if no one lived to bury him, how would he reach the otherworld? She could not shake from her mind the fear that her mother would not find him, that she could not make sure he was lowered into the earth with due ceremony. How would he be laid to rest with his sword and shield, honoured as he deserved?

The other fear, for her mother and for Sparrow, was threaded with faint hope. They could not all have died. Not every man, woman and child. There must have been survivors, like herself but free, waking to a new day beyond the ashes of the dead village. Why should the two people she loved most not be among them?

Never had she imagined that a journey could be so endless. Hunger gnawed inside her but the thirst was worse, and there were those around her who could not go much further. One girl, not much older than herself, slept deeply nearby. Hours later she slept on silently, and did not stir when the blunt end of a soldier's spear began to prod her. Aifa watched as she was rolled over roughly with the aid of a kicking foot. Wide eyes stared up raw with tears and flame, but still as stone. Aifa turned her own eyes away. It was the first death of the journey, but not the last.

Afterwards, Aifa had little sense of how far they had travelled. She only remembered more than one pitch-black night in the cart, which stopped somewhere for the soldiers to rest. For the captives there was no food, no chance to stretch their legs and no clue to where they might be. Exhaustion gave her the only respite she could hope for from a kind of numb, deadened terror. But her sleep was troubled, fitful and soaked with sweat.

The other captives in the wagon were unfamiliar, apart from one, a tall boy from her settlement. She had always been too shy to talk to him, and he too old and proud to speak to her. Even now he only scowled at her, grim and silent. His leg bled, and she saw how much it hurt him. Most of the time he hugged it to him, his chin on his knees, and when he wiped the blood away with a corner of his cloak, it only seeped out again. Aifa did not know, with no herbs and no water, how to help him, but she tried, with her eyes, to show him that she prayed for him. She fingered the beauty of Epona around her neck and hoped he knew.

Even the soldiers seemed concerned when the boy grew yellow-white in morning light. Two of them looked at him, muttered their strange grunts, and looked angry. Then they took him by the shoulders and dragged him to his feet. Before Aifa had begun to understand, they had thrown him from the wagon like a stack of corn or an armful of firewood.

"No!" she cried, watching him land motionless on rocky ground, feeling his pain.

A hand struck her cheek, drew a bead of blood from the corner of her mouth. The soldier stood over her, the fist ready should she ask for more. She looked away from it and from his cruel face, sitting down while she still had the strength to choose. The boy's blood was fresh beside her, a red flower blossoming as it soaked into the straw.

"Bullies," she murmured, in a whisper they could not hear. "Cowards," she added, and closed her eyes.

When they finally reached their destination, Aifa saw little of the town over the top of the cart. When she tried to stand and peer out, she was beaten back down onto the straw. But she saw enough to know that she had come a long way from home.

All she had known until that day was her own settlement and the country that lay within a day's walk of it. Of course, her father had spoken more than once of hill forts, fenced villages built high above any enemies who might seek to attack. Such forts, he said, enclosed homes for more families than she had ever met. But this was no such place. It was larger still, and growing. That much she could tell from the barrage of sound that bombarded them, turn after turn, street after street.

Along with the unintelligible speech swelling around her, there was from time to time the clink of iron that reminded her of her father at work, shaping tools in fire. This town was not yet finished. And there were so many voices! Many of them were raised, but some also gathered in conversation, for she heard the lilt of friendliness, and one or two outbreaks of laughter.

Familiar through the other sounds flowed the evidence of water, the tugging of boats pulling a channel through it, the cries of the birds that lived beside it, and the unmistakeable smell of its life and its decay. This town had a river running through it.

The journey came to an end in a market place overlooked by unfamiliar buildings. Stumbling out of the cart, her legs unsteady, she gazed around her in amazement, putting pictures to some of the noises, and glaring at the soldier who pushed her out onto a kind of wooden podium. Her wrists still tied behind her bruised back, she was told to stand tall and straight. Not that she understood the sharp words. It was the spear between her shoulder blades that communicated the message.

She was lined up with many others, all of them roped and some of them no older than herself, but others strong, fully grown men. Standing tall, their pride made them bristle or scowl and she felt their shame, their loss of dignity. Would not her father shout and shove, wrestle and kick? Would he not throw them all off and fight?

But of course they had no chance and no choice. One captive who did not co-operate was beaten savagely. A whip with many tails tore through his tunic, while a small crowd gathered to jeer. A fine spray of blood spattered those who were closest, but they did not move. Amongst them, Aifa saw families as well as soldiers. Their faces were strange, and their eyes, when they rested on her, showed no feeling.

The soldiers she saw around her were smarter and cleaner than the bullies who had poked and kicked, and thrown a boy to die. In their heavy helmets and breastplates they were just as her friend the fish seller had described them, but today they were not part of a machine. Some looked casual rather than drilled as they talked and laughed, grouped to drink from a well.

But there were other men, who wore no armour but stood proudly in long draping robes that had not trailed in dirt or crusted with blood. Aifa did not need to hear the rattle of their coins to know that these were the rich and powerful. Not soldiers, but leaders of some kind. Their hair was shaved short and their skin soft. She saw too that close beside them waited others in rougher, dirtier tunics, ready to do their bidding. They did not speak unless spoken to, and bowed to their masters, quick and eager to please, but even more afraid to fail.

Such a Roman master was the man who bought her, clean, smooth-chinned and softly spoken. He looked her over, all over, but a step away, too far for her to smell him or too far for him to prod a leg or lift her chin. He did not speak, and though he fixed his gaze on her, on every part of her, she made quite sure his eyes never met hers. It was as if she were of no more interest than a clay pot or a wooden chest. Like them she must be inspected for imperfections. And though it seemed he found no fault in her, she felt no satisfaction. What she felt was more like shame.

Those hard, judging eyes rested on her longer than on any other girl he might have chosen instead, and returned to her once more after they had turned away to compare her with the others. She knew she'd been chosen, even before he nodded to her and spoke to the man in charge, the trader who had done the deal that made them his to sell. But she didn't know how to feel.

Something in the reaction of the auctioneers, and the hostile stares of the other captives lined up with her, told her that the price this man had paid for her was high. She heard it repeated through the crowd, like a surprise, but it was a number that, like this town and the foreign people in it, meant nothing to her.

33

Though she could think of no possible reason why she should be worth more than any other miserable captive, still she felt no pride. It was all more humiliating than she wanted to remember. And nowhere, in the eyes of any of the slaves who washed her roughly and threw a tunic over her head, was there a glimmer of kindness. It seemed as if she were no longer a person but a tool, being prepared for others to use her.

The money counted, Aifa was led like a dog by a rope around her wrists, not by the smooth-skinned man but by some kind of servant. He seemed to be more than a slave, and made sure she knew it, spitting near her feet as they walked and sneering as he jerked the rope. Walking past stalls selling fresh bread, herbs and spices, meat and fruit, she felt the ache of hunger, but had no illusions that she might be fed. Her mouth was so dry it felt sharp. As she was dragged past some buckets full of water she cried out, and leaned her head towards them, her eyes pleading, till he frowned but stopped. She scooped some handfuls of the cool water into her mouth, and was still reaching back for more when he pulled the rope and moved her on.

The house where he took her was on the edge of the town, away from the noise. It was built round its own courtyard and set in the beginnings of a young garden scented with herbs. Aifa lifted her eyes to take in the reach of it. But for all its size, she had expected more, something finer and grander than the timber frame underneath the plaster, something rather less smoky.

She was washed, unceremoniously, and dressed in a plain but clean brown tunic that felt crisp against her skin. Then, at last, she was fed with a kind of porridge, and a torn crust of hardening bread. But the eating was hurried and joyless, in an enormous, sweaty kitchen full of steam and pungent aromas, heat and grease. She barely had time to swallow the last bite before she was taken across the courtyard into a room that smelt of flowers, where the plaster was painted white. There she was to be inspected by her Roman mistress, the Lady Claudia.

It was the long, jewelled neck she saw first, dark hair trailing in elaborate curls onto one shoulder. The face that looked her over as she turned was the first lovely face Aifa had seen since she'd lost sight of the dear faces she missed most. But there was not so much as a flicker of a smile on the painted red mouth, or in the cold eyes that lingered on her.

"There is nothing to fear," she said, "if you are good – if you are obedient and loyal." She looked questioningly at Aifa, who stared down at her bare feet. "Are you obedient and loyal?" But she answered her own question. "Of course you are! I can see it in your eyes."

So Aifa had no chance to consider her answer, to lie or choose sullen silence. She simply stood, as tall and proud as a tiny girl could stand after days with little food, water or clean air. She blanked her face and deadened her eyes. Her self became a secret she must hide.

Yet over the weeks that followed, the assumption her mistress had made in that first encounter turned out to be true. She was a good slave; she couldn't help it. She had been a good daughter. Now she found herself submitting, silently, humbly, to every rule. She told the Lady Claudia her name when asked, though it felt like betrayal. She even repeated it, to help her mistress pronounce it correctly, and she answered to it at once, like a well-trained dog. And as the days went by, and she learned more about what the life of a slave could mean, she realised how fortunate she was to be called by that name, by any name. It was something that the lowest, the least worthy in the eyes of these Roman masters, were denied.

In the kitchens where she worked, chopping and scrubbing, her stomach heaving with the smell of fish sauce bubbling day after day, the others barely spoke to her. She felt them glare and scowl in her direction, heard them mutter. But the enemy of her people, the mistress from Rome, never failed to give her the smallest but gentlest of smiles when she poured her wine or held the bowl where she dipped her fingers.

Knowing nothing of the languages of the British tribes, Claudia tried to teach Aifa a little of the Latin which she spoke with her husband. And Aifa found that though her heart resisted, her mind absorbed the words, shaped the sentences and privately enjoyed the rhythmic cadence of the speech. She learned quickly, and her mistress seemed delighted to discover how much she understood.

As each new darkness fell, when she lay trying to banish from her tired mind the smoke-filled, screaming village, Aifa would reach, night after night, for the horse around her neck. The copper necklace no longer hung cold against her skin, but every time she felt it gone, she imagined its shape, its feel. She would not have parted with it for all the gold in the hills, but she had known, from the moment of her capture, what she must do.

All through the cart ride and the auction, she had clasped it tightly in her clenched fist, and then, on her first long morning of steam and oil and threatened beatings, she had slipped it into a crack in the kitchen wall. As she left it there, and walked away without daring to look back, she had felt a knot of sadness. But she was glad. Her mother would be proud, for now no Roman hand would tear it from her neck, or mock it with a sneer.

But this small, furtive deception had been her last, secret defiance. She was glad her father could not see her, nodding, accepting, drinking in their language till it began to flow in her. She was afraid he would scorn her meek obedience, and disown her for what she had become: a spineless traitor.

Her mistress was pleased with her effortless progress, and when she was not ignoring her seemed to amuse herself by calling her name. It was as if she wished to test and increase Aifa's new understanding.

"Aifa," she would say, "which colour today?" and with an elegant sweep of her bare, gold-ringed arm, she showed her the gowns in softly draping fabric carefully laid across her bed – the green, the lilac, the blue.

"Aifa," she would order her, from that bed, when she had not yet seen fit to rise, "pick flowers to fill this vase. These are tired and their scent is thick. It pains my head."

"Aifa," she would call her, from one room to another, imperious and impatient, "find me my snake ring. It's missing and I'm told it's nowhere to be found."

So she spent less and less time scrubbing and chopping, and more and more under the glare of the Lady Claudia's handmaidens, in her bedroom and with her in the gardens. Sometimes she thought the cold and discontented lady, who often spoke of her own country with sadness and longing, forgot who it was she was talking to. It was as if she were so lost in her memories that she took Aifa for a high-born Roman girl, rather than a savage, an ill-mannered, uneducated, artless slave. It was strange and confusing.

Aifa listened as she must, nodded when she needed to, and learned to shape a little, compliant smile. She could not eat as she used to eat. Neither could she speak, sleep or work as she used to do, or pay respect to Epona except in the silence of her private heart. But she had forgotten nothing.

Chapter Five

Chicken Legs

It was a month or more before the routine of Aifa's days was broken by the arrival of an angry Roman boy in a short white tunic. Didius, who had cropped hair, and long thin legs that reminded her of a chicken, was the only son of her master and mistress. And it was hard to find one reason not to dislike him deeply.

Being highborn, he imagined himself very fine and liked to show how important he was by shouting at the slaves. But though Aifa nodded and obeyed, she scorned his manners – or lack of them. He shrugged and sulked and mumbled when his mother instructed him, and often scowled at her back, gesticulating rudely. Aifa, who had never been disrespectful to a mother who loved her, was shocked to hear him raise his voice to Claudia when she blocked his strong, greedy will.

As for Aifa, it was not long before he told her exactly what she was.

"You're less than a hunting dog," he sneered, as she offered him the heavy bowl of fruit. "My father was swindled when he paid for you, and if I were him, I'd demand my denarii back."

Aifa only stood, waiting patiently, her eyes fixed firmly on the fruit.

"This apple is rotten," he hissed in her ear, and pushed the mouldy skin against her nose, laughing as she drew her head away. "The maggots remind me of you. Look at the way you squirm."

He picked one such wriggling creature, or pretended to, and trawled it across her hair – till his mother spoke his name in a sharp, hurt voice. It was a voice she had never yet used with Aifa, slave or no slave...

"You should beat her, Mother," he called across the room as she turned to rejoin her guests. "She's lazy. They're all lazy. And they smell."

Like Claudia, who ignored his rudeness, Aifa made no reply, although she was quickly learning the stiff language these Romans spoke. Instead she boldly turned on him an unflinching stare that told him she felt no fear and no humility. He thought he was better than her, but her eyes told him he was wrong.

Bored with everything, he sighed, threw the apple on the ground, and swaggered away. Aifa, marvelling at those bony legs, clucked silently, and allowed herself a real and secret smile.

It seemed to Aifa that Didius had hated her on sight, but something happened soon afterwards that made him resent her even more.

His father, who had bought Aifa, was a soldier of high rank, but he was also a man of law. More often than not, he left home carrying not a sword but long scrolls marked with lettering. Didius boasted that he was a frequent guest at the palace.

"He's a legatus juridicus," he told her, enjoying the long words and her blank incomprehension. "Not that you know what that means. You know nothing. You know less than the mice they stuff in the kitchens!"

Aifa made sure that her face, indeed, told him nothing. But he was not looking into her thoughts, only beating her with his own.

"He advises Suetonius Paulinus, who is, for your information, brainless slave, the governor of Britannia. The whole of this grey, wet country of yours!"

He told her that the governor received his orders directly from the Emperor in Rome.

"The Emperor! Have you no idea of his power? That people live and die at his orders? He's almost a god. And he listens to a man who listens to *my* father!"

So his father, he told her, was a very important man. And like all important men, he wanted only the best for his son, however little he deserved it. Claudia told Aifa, who scarcely began to understand what she meant, that Didius was to receive an education. He was to learn the things that a high-born Roman needed to know. Aifa simply listened. She would have liked to know whether they included common courtesy.

When a tutor arrived from Rome to teach Didius in his own home, he was pleased enough, until he discovered that his mother had spoken to his teacher about another pupil – who needed a different kind of education.

"My mother's wits are failing!" he raged at Aifa, throwing his writing tablet at her.

Aifa did not even need to duck to avoid the missile. His aim was so weak that he would never have managed, in her village, to knock the bread from a post. How ashamed her father would have been of such a son! And she smiled to herself, imagining the terrible punishments his precious Roman army would inflict on any soldier who fell so pitifully short of a target.

"Don't smirk at me, slave!" he yelled. "My mother is mistaken if she thinks that learning to read and write will make you civilised. You are nothing, and you will always be nothing."

Learning to read! Aifa did not understand how it worked, how the marks on the page carried a mysterious meaning, but she had seen these Romans, the powerful ones, reading from their scrolls, making their own marks with copper pens, or, like Didius, carving with a stylus in wax. She did not know what wonderful things the marks would reveal to her. She felt sure that they would change her, whatever Didius said, but she would never let them make her one of them.

"Can the Lady Claudia read?" she wondered, because she had never seen it.

"She's a woman! Why would she need to read?"

But if it was such a stupid question, the answer made even less sense. Why should Aifa, a female slave, be given knowledge that her mistress lacked?

She determined to ask the tutor, the obliging Septimus, as soon as she had the chance. He was old, but so eager it made her like him at once. It was clear that the knowledge he had to share excited him, just as the beauty of shooting a bird excited Didius. A small, stocky man with bright eyes and an animated way of talking, she overheard that he had once been a slave but was now a free man.

A slave like her! It was hard to understand or believe. So there was a way of escaping the drudgery! But not, it seemed, without surrendering pride. Unlike the well-bred Didius, he had perfect manners, and a natural smile. But if she, Aifa, felt like a traitor to her people, what did his position among these Romans make him? How could he live with his comfort when he had bought it by turning his back on everything he was and all that he loved – his people, his language, his gods?

If he was surprised to be tutoring a slave, and a girl at that, Septimus did not show it. He treated her with simple kindness. Aifa couldn't help marvelling, wide-eyed, when he sat down by the window beside her and unrolled a long and detailed map on the table. As he showed her Britannia, she saw her own country, marked with the name of her tribe, and told him that this was where she belonged.

He pointed to Rome, too, and the seas that separated them, the seas he had crossed in a small boat rowed by soldiers. He described the voyage and the storm that had nearly sunk the ship and drowned him. She found herself smiling up at him in amazement, and he smiled back, grateful for a pupil who listened to him, and did not sulk.

But she soon discovered that unlike Didius, who read fluently in the stiff Latin language that was beginning to unravel its mystery as she listened to it, Aifa was not to learn to read.

"It's as I said!" jeered Didius. "Girls are not fit for lettering or numerals. Their brains are too small. They need only learn to simper and sing, dance and sew, and pretend they are goddesses when they have no power at all."

He did not know that Septimus had no interest in teaching her such things. Her lessons consisted of more challenging ideas than how to style hair or stand like a lady. Didius would have flown into a fury had he seen the maps, the diagrams, the pictures of birds and stars, the poetry she was allowed to hear. She was a quick learner. Soon the tutor had good reports for Claudia, who gave her a stuffed date from the dish beside her bed when Aifa came to unpin her hair. It was sweet, but spicy, and seeing that she liked it, Claudia offered her another.

"Thank you, mistress," she said, and ate it slowly, fooling herself that it could help to ward off the hunger that she felt every evening through till morning.

"You are my favourite, you know," said Claudia, stroking her hair and playing with it, as if considering how she could style it for her.

"I know," said Aifa. She paused a moment. "But why?"

In a moment her hair had fallen down to her shoulders again, and her mistress's back was turned.

"Go now," she told her, suddenly cold with sadness.

When Aifa asked Septimus, he tried to change the subject. Then he told her that he could not say; it was no business of his. However well-educated he had become through his own wits and effort, he was mindful of his humble beginnings and his place in the household. It was not for him to gossip about the affairs of his master and mistress. But she persisted.

"I am not stupid, sir," she told him. "Slaves do not have tutors. Slaves do not receive their lady's smiles, or their lady's food. And I do not believe her wits are failing her…"

"No indeed!"

"Then I beg you, sir, to tell me, that I may understand."

Septimus looked thoughtfully at her earnest expression, drew a short breath, and explained that two years after Didius was born, the Lady Claudia had given birth to an unexpectedly fair little girl whom she named Livia. She died suddenly when she was seven years old.

"You remind her of her lost daughter," he said, "and it comforts her to be with you. But, Aifa, be warned. It also makes her sad – and no one wants to be sad for ever."

"No," said Aifa. "I know."

She had already told him she wasn't stupid. She knew that her mistress might wake one day and decide to banish the living, breathing reminder of her heartbreak. No one needed an education to work out what that could mean.

Chapter Six

The Pupil

Aifa had never realised how little she knew. Of course she knew a great deal that was useful, patient and practical, but not much about anything she couldn't make or eat – or use to make Claudia feel more beautiful. And she wasn't sure anyone had the expertise required to make her mistress happy.

Now, however, she was learning new thoughts every day. Without exactly disobeying his orders, Septimus opened her eyes to a wider world full of ideas and wondering as well as facts. While he did not actually teach her to recognise letters or numerals, he used dates and verse, astronomy and geography to help her learn. All the ideas Didius hated, struggled with and dismissed as stupid, came easily to Aifa.

And because Septimus had once been powerless like her, he understood the power that knowledge had given him. He just wasn't sure that Aifa was ready to accept it – or anything else that came from a Roman mind.

"Give them up, child!" he coaxed her. "All those rebellious thoughts of yours!" he told her. "Stop resisting. Forget your anger and that sense of injustice. None of it will help you. It will only hold you back."

Like he had done before her, she should work hard, he said, be humble and study her way to some kind of independence.

"Don't you see," he asked her, "that if you don't stop playing the victim you will never be free?"

"I survive," she cried, insulted. "I wait. I hope."

He nodded, and patted her hand as it lay closed on the table.

"As I did. But you don't think I am free," he said, "do you?"

Aifa liked him, respected him – and did not understand him. She looked away.

"Freedom," he said, "lies here," and he held a loose fist to his chest, close to his heartbeat.

Aifa tried to smile. But she was not ready to give up hope of a better, open-air kind of freedom with familiar smells and voices that she did not need to translate. Or the freedom that comes from loving and being loved.

Claudia teased her that she was a little lady now, sewing, reciting the poetry she had learned by heart, counting her mistress's ribbons and rings in Latin.

"You were a wild creature," she smiled. "And now…look at what you have become."

"I do not forget my people," she said, daring to lift her eyes, "that I belong to the Silures, and that I am the daughter of a great man."

Claudia's smile faded equally quickly.

"And my slave," she added, quietly.

Not in my heart, thought Aifa. In my heart I am free. But a tear choked the silent voice inside her as she pictured her father's body in the burning village, her mother clasping Acco to her and running for their lives.

"Don't be sad, child."

Claudia reached out, and stroked her hair from her face. Aifa stared up at her, startled and rigid.

"You are more than a slave to me," her mistress added gently. "And you have no need to fear me."

She took Aifa's chin in her hand and turned her face towards hers.

"You must learn to trust me, for I will never hurt you."

Perhaps she could tell that Aifa was not so sure. With a sigh of disappointment she let go of her, directed her to a heavy weight of robes for the laundry and sent her away with them.

So huge was the layered pile across her arms that it was difficult to carry without walking blinded into a sudden pillar. Aware of a trailing corner of favourite green loosened to the puddled ground in the courtyard, she tried to retrieve it while balancing the bulk against her chest. A wet black stain would not endear her to the slaves in the laundry – or to Claudia, when her carelessness was reported. As she struggled to keep her load under control she saw, in a corner, another brown tunic bending like her own, as the girl inside it folded like the garments. And crumpled again, knocked aside with a faint moan.

She saw whose arm had struck. It rested threatening in the air as if it might be ready, like an onager in the kind of battle he liked to recount, to kick back and fire again. Aifa did not know the slave girl's name. But she knew the arm even before the voice, grinding into a shout. She looked for a moment at the robes before she let them fall to the ground beside the fountain.

Aifa ran. Didius turned at the sound of her feet, challenged her with a stare that was almost a smile, and turned back to the cowering girl, her face bloody, fallen against a sapling bright-leaved in the morning sun. Aifa placed herself between them, the shaking girl and the boy with his arm still raised and ready. For a moment she thought he was going to throw back his head and laugh. Then the mouth that had begun to sneer set hard around clenched teeth, and his hands tightened in two fists. But Didius did not move. Aifa realised, with a flutter of surprise, that he did not know what to do.

"Stop now," she said, very quietly, as if she were talking to Sparrow, as if what he needed was soothing.

It was the girl who stopped, her body stilling and her whimpers ebbing away. Aifa turned from him, and helped her to her feet. She half-expected to be knocked down once her back was turned, but as she looked into the girl's cut face she heard him go, his marching steps gathering into a run as he disappeared into the house.

The girl tried to smile, but pain cut her short. Aifa bathed her face with water from the fountain. Then she picked up half the clothes from the ground.

"Help me?" said Aifa, offering the armful.

They walked in silence to the laundry, left their loads without a word, and parted outside. As she walked away, the girl stopped long enough to tell Aifa that her name was Brigit.

"I'm a Catevellauni."

"Aifa..." she began.

"I know who you are," Brigit told her. "Everyone does."

When Aifa returned to Claudia as summoned, she waited outside the bedroom as instructed. The door opened. Didius brushed past her, turned, jabbed a finger towards her eye like a spear, as if he would be glad to gouge it out, and muttered, very slowly, between his teeth.

"My mother is a soft sow – and you've bewitched her somehow, you little..." He lowered his hand into the familiar fist. "But she'll sing a different song when my father returns."

He walked away, throwing after him an invitation to Aifa to wait, and a promise that she would soon be sorry. Watching him go, Aifa gathered her breath, knocked and entered.

Claudia wanted her hair brushed. Again. She liked it better, she said, when Aifa did it, than in any other hands.

"Pretty hands," she said quietly, and sighed.

She did not speak again until the hair was curled and piled, the comb in place, and Aifa dismissed. And as Aifa drifted into sleep that night, she pictured chicken legs in preference to teeth and fists.

Whether he was avoiding her, or whether Epona were protecting her, Didius had no opportunity over the weeks that followed to take revenge of any kind. But every day Aifa listened for clues that might herald the return of the father of whom even Claudia was supposed to be afraid.

As the weeks went by, however, and the weather warmed and brightened, the news that stirred through the town like a biting, whirling wind was of someone else. Aifa was the last to hear, of course, and when she did, it was from Septimus, his eagerness gone and an anxious frown creasing his forehead.

"You have heard of Boudicca, Queen of the Iceni?"

"I don't know," she said, at first, because there were so many groups within so many tribes, and so many kings and queens.

But then she remembered something her father had said about Boudicca's husband, Prasutagus, the Iceni king. "Traitor!" was her father's judgement, because he had died leaving half of everything he owned to the Romans.

Her mother had suggested that he must have done it for his family and his people – to protect them and keep the peace. But to the men of the Silures there was no excuse for such wheedling treachery.

It seemed, however, that his plan to keep the peace had not worked as well as he'd hoped.

"She has raised an army," Septimus told Aifa, "attacked the town of Camulodonum. She burned it to the ground. They killed many…too many to count, and not just soldiers, but women and children too!"

Aifa tried not to hear the screams.

"They are calling her a witch, a devil, a madwoman," continued Septimus. "But I say she is nothing but an evil savage, a barbarian who will be destroyed, and forgotten."

Aifa couldn't think clearly about Boudicca. Her mind was full of flames. She was running through choking smoke, and stumbling over corpses she dared not see.

Chapter Seven

A Friend

Claudia was entertaining guests, and far too busy to concern herself with her pet slave. For the first time in weeks, Aifa had been sent to the kitchens. She had forgotten the smells: the sweat and oil, bodies and sauces. She quickly remembered how hard the work was. The heat was steamy and oppressive. They were allowed little rest, and breathed no air that wasn't thick with fat. Roman guests, it seemed, never had enough to eat. And sometimes they ate so much they hurled the food back to the floor, in a puddle of soupy vomit. The first time Aifa had cleaned it away, she had very nearly added to it with some sick of her own.

Now, in the kitchens, the slaves were talking about the same queen that Septimus had named, and the same victory. Their faces grew damp and red as they roasted a pig on the spit.

"They say she is brave as a she-wolf protecting her young," said one.

"We are all courageous," said the slave from Gaul. "Courage is not enough, not against these people. She will be captured, and then she will die."

"Better to die than live like this," muttered another, staring the crisping, sizzling pig in its dead, round eye as it spun slowly round to face him. "Unless, of course," he added pointedly, "you are a favourite of the enemy."

He scowled up from the pig to Aifa, who was stirring the fish sauce, still appalled that any living being could stomach it. She held herself as tall as she could, given that most of them dwarfed her. They must see that she was not cowed. And she was not ashamed.

"My father said he'd heard Boudicca is tall as a man," she told them. "But her hair falls in wild waves."

A cold moment of silence greeted Aifa's speech. She rarely talked with the other slaves, preferring to busy herself quietly. That way, she hoped, they would scarcely notice she existed.

She knew, too, that they did not trust her. They probably expected her to spy on them and report back to her mistress. Perhaps they thought her announcement was some kind of trap to ensnare them. No one looked at her and no one seemed inclined to respond, until the girl on the other side of the table did both.

"I heard her voice is deep and strong as thunder," said the girl.

Aifa looked up, her face blank in spite of the lift of her heart inside. She had not seen her through the steam. Brigit's face had healed.

"I would like to hear her speak," ventured Aifa. "I would like to see her for myself."

Brigit met her gaze.

"Yes," she said. "I would too."

It was not quite a smile that passed between them, but it was close.

"Such nonsense about this Boudicca!" cried the slave from Gaul, skinning something Aifa hoped was not a mouse. "She could be a goddess for all the good it will do her."

He headed towards the gathering laughter with a jug to fill enemy glasses.

"More work, less chatter!" came a shout.

The cook's cry was sharp, but the glare for Aifa, as she hurried to fill a finger bowl, was sharper. Aifa knew now that, away from the elegance of Claudia's bedroom, being the favourite of the mistress meant more work, and more shoves and slaps for her, than for any other skivvy in the sweltering kitchen. She had the feeling that if any guest was neglected or dissatisfied, it would be her fault and earn her a beating.

She saw Brigit struggling with three dishes, one of which was laden with fruit. Without a word she held out her hand to help, and this time the smile was brief but warm.

"Thank you, Aifa," she muttered.

They walked into the banquet together, dismayed by the drunkenness that swelled around them as they entered. They grimaced privately at one another, sharing a mocking disapproval. It was madness, a reckless risk to take, but it helped, sometimes, to laugh at these Romans even while they feared them.

Though the master was away with the army, it didn't stop his friends feasting and carousing in his name. Claudia, a natural hostess, made sure of that. Her husband might be risking his life for the Roman Empire, but this evening looked set to be as long and loud as any other.

Back in the kitchens between tasks, Aifa dared to speak to Brigit about the master.

"He has a gentle face and good manners. His voice holds authority, and he's clever," she muttered. "But he must have been responsible for killing fathers like yours and mine – for defending their homes and families!"

Brigit looked shocked. She cast her eyes around for listening ears that might betray them. Aifa spoke with her usual quietness, but she was warming to her subject. It was such a puzzle. He was a man of education. Yet she presumed that when he returned home from battle, and lay peacefully in the steaming water of a hot bath, he left Celtic bodies lying in the dirt behind him.

"They're not like us," said Brigit simply.

"But they're only human too." Aifa paused. "Well, with one exception. And he's a chicken. Have you seen his legs?"

It took a moment, but a shocked smile spread on Brigit's face. Then she considered.

"She's as bad," she said, with feeling. "She has no heart."

56

Brigit did not dare say Claudia's name, but Aifa knew who she meant. She had felt her mistress's coldness, but she also knew she had felt love, for the daughter she missed so much.

"She doesn't miss the master," she agreed. "I wonder if she even fears for him when he's fighting."

Later that night, as Aifa held the dish for Claudia to dip her elegant white, jewelled fingers between courses, she watched her mistress's face. She laughed, loudly. Her eyes were bright. Aifa could see no anxiety, no sign that this rich Roman wife loved her husband. Not, at least, as her mother had loved her father. And thinking of her own parents made her eyes cloud and sting.

Aifa's sudden tear fell just in the moment when her mistress looked up. Surely she must have seen it, trickling unwiped from a corner of one eye? But there was nothing in her flirtatious, drunken laughter, as she leaned towards the young poet to feed him grapes one by one, to suggest that she cared. Her kind words meant nothing. Perhaps Brigit was right about the space where her heart should be.

Later that night, her duties over, Aifa longed to settle down to sleep. Running her fingers through her thick hair in a vain attempt to unravel the tangles, she was startled to find Claudia at her shoulder, a little unsteady and rather flushed.

"Don't be sad, Livia," she slurred. "I believe... I truly believe the gods sent you to me."

Aifa stared in blank incomprehension. Livia! Her mistress must be very drunk indeed.

"The moment you came to us, I saw her in your eyes. You are a gift from the gods, an answer to my prayers, and one day soon, when I have finished preparing you, we will convince him, and he will accept you too…"

She took Aifa's hand and led her to the shrine in honour of the goddess Juno, where rose petals had been scattered at the foot of the little statue.

"Give thanks with me," she said, her eyes bright, and fell to her knees.

Aifa looked at the carving, at the firm folds of her robes and the hard curls of her hair. She heard her mother's voice, telling her to trust Epona, and she knew she could not betray either of them. She stood, still as the goddess herself.

And then, as Claudia swayed and sighed, and reached for a pillar to steady herself, Aifa ran. She did not stop until she had reached the courtyard, where she drew breath, and hid in the shadows beneath the moon. She felt the skin heave at her neck, and longed to touch the horse that used to rest cool against it.

"O great Epona," she whispered, "save me."

Chapter Eight

Leaving

Perhaps it was chance that saved her, but she liked to believe it was Epona.

The following day she was told that Claudia was leaving town, and that she, Aifa, had been chosen to attend her. She would accompany her mistress, along with Septimus and a particularly grumpy Didius. But no one seemed to know where or why.

First Claudia told her that they were to take very little with them. Then when Aifa started to pack only a few of her finest gowns, leaving the others on the bed, she protested.

"Aifa!" she cried. "Do you want to break my heart?"

Nothing could separate Claudia from her jewellery. She seemed bad-tempered. Aifa decided that she had a very sore head, and no wish to go anywhere.

The kitchen was busy as more than a little food was prepared for the journey. As she wrapped it, Aifa asked the same question of everyone, to find that no one knew the reason for their departure. But Aifa did not sense any panic. And, judging from the curtness of the answers, Aifa gathered that some of the other slaves seemed resentful that once again she was the chosen one.

Putting her curiosity aside, along with a fear that seemed second nature to her now, she began instead to feel a thrill. After months of imprisonment in this house and this city, she was about to leave.

But Claudia was far from excited. She was so quiet and distracted that Aifa wondered whether she even remembered the conversation of the previous evening. She was brisk with her, but called her by her own name and made no mention of the goddess Juno until, when they were almost ready to leave, she made a final visit to the shrine. But to Aifa's relief, she did not press her to accompany her.

At last! Aifa took the chance to hurry back to the kitchens, volunteering to fetch olives for the journey. Finding only three slaves in her way, she told them Claudia needed them in the gardens. Then she reached into to the crack in the wall where her fingers felt the copper horse waiting. She took a deep breath, and rubbed it thankfully.

"Aifa! What are you doing?"

It was Brigit. Aifa held the necklace tight inside her palm.

"Nothing."

"You are leaving with the mistress?"

"Yes. I wish…"

Aifa wished she had the time to test this friendship, new as it was, to see if it was real.

"Will you be away long?"

"I don't know."

"I'll miss you," said the girl, and smiled shyly. "Don't talk to anyone else as you talked to me. It isn't safe."

"No."

She would go back to her silence, to watching and thinking. She would be alone again.

To her surprise, Brigit kissed her cheek, quickly and lightly, before she lifted an amphora of olive oil and carried it out of the kitchen.

"Goodbye," Aifa called after her.

"Goodbye," came Brigit's voice. "The gods be with you."

Alone again, Aifa wrapped a long ribbon round the necklace of Epona and tied the ribbon round her narrow waist. She must hurry. She hoped she had not been missed. The tiny copper horse bounced off her thigh as she moved. She was glad to feel its presence with her in every step.

She returned to find Didius in the foulest of moods.

"Where have you been, scum? Where are the olives?"

She had forgotten them! Her mouth opened but he did not want to hear her excuses.

"You are as much use as a slug in a chariot race!" he jeered. "Here! Quickly! And don't drop them in the dirt or I'll have you whipped!"

He thrust a bundle of clothes into her arms, then watched idly and impatiently as Aifa loaded the wagon. Septimus, who was to drive the horses that would pull it, while mother and son sat inside, came to help her.

"Why does she have to come?" Didius asked him, nodding towards Aifa.

"To attend your mother," he told him.

"I suppose she needs someone," he conceded, "but why does it have to be her?"

He scowled at Aifa, who should have had the sense to keep her head down, attending to her bending and carrying, but didn't. Instead of averting her eyes, she lifted them, and held him in the utter contempt of a quick but icy stare.

"She's insolent!" he cried furiously. "She has no shame!"

"Perhaps," said his tutor, almost too quietly for him to hear, "she has nothing to be ashamed of."

"My choice of companion is not a subject for discussion," said Claudia, appearing in her cloak anxious to begin the journey. "I have my fearless son to protect me, a wise man to advise me and my best, useful girl to serve me."

"I will ride," announced Didius. "I want my horse with me."

He had, in fact, no horse of his own, but would not be denied. He marched off to commandeer the finest.

"But where are we going?" Aifa murmured to the tutor, who only shrugged his shoulders and climbed up to take the reins.

He was about to lift Aifa up beside him when Claudia protested.

"Let her sit inside with me. I must have some company."

Aifa could only comply with her whim and climb in. She had no wish to be there, but at least she could enjoy imagining the rage it would provoke in Didius when he returned on horseback to find her sitting beside his mother.

He did not disappoint, but his mother told him that if he did not like the arrangement he could ride off and make his own way without them. Frowning, and snorting in an impression of the mare, he whipped the animal into a canter and announced that he would lead.

As they set off, Claudia asked Aifa if she was comfortable.

"Thank you, mistress. I am."

"I do not delude myself you will spare me many words to pass the time," Claudia told her, "but you, at least, are civil. Unlike certain highborn young men who have not yet learned respect."

The wagon gathered speed. They approached the outskirts of the town, the soldiers on guard standing statue-stiff for them to pass. Then they raced away from Londinium along the new road that reached straight as a Roman javelin ahead of them.

"We are to visit my sister Flavia," Claudia told her. "Her husband is building a grand estate in the country – and mine, for his own reasons, has sent word that I am to stay there in their new villa." She paused. "Flavia will be glad to impress. Even as a child she threw a tantrum if she couldn't beat me at knucklebones."

Aifa smiled. She was good at that herself.

"I care for my sister rather less than I care for you," continued Claudia, "but she is my sister nonetheless."

It was alarming. Aifa, who would have loved to share the closeness of sisters, did not understand. The words filled her head with questions.

"Don't worry," said Claudia. "If she wants to play the mad empress and behead slaves, she'll have to pick on her own!"

Aifa did not join in the laughter – slightly mad itself – that followed. She was busy sensing the sounds and smells that helped her to imagine where they were. And as time passed, she knew that they had left the town behind for the scent of grass and flowers, and the animal life thick in the shadows.

The country! What did that mean? Away from Londinium, but how far beyond? Were they heading north perhaps, into a colder, bleaker landscape further yet from the life she used to know? Or was it possible – was there the slenderest of chances – that they might head west, in the direction of the country of the Silures?

Of course they would never venture far into the unmapped wilds of a land the Romans deemed too primitive to conquer.

But to think that they might travel close by, yet never close enough, was torture. And if they did, if her mother should be nearby – enslaved or free, healthy or sick, alone or tending baby Sparrow – how would she know? How could she find them?

Chapter Nine

Inferno

Sleep spared Aifa the awkwardness of conversation with her mistress. Claudia, still suffering the effects of the wine, closed her eyes first, and Aifa soon followed. But they had travelled only a few miles when they drew to a sudden stop. As soon as her eyes opened, Aifa knew something was wrong. The horses were agitated, listening.

"Wait!" cried Didius. "Wait here!"

He beat his horse into a gallop and headed back in the direction they had come, up to the brow of a small hill, where they had stopped the wagon only minutes before to look down on the city.

As she shivered in the chilling air, in spite of the fur her mistress allowed her to share, Aifa tasted in her mouth the familiar bitterness of smoke. A cold fist of fear gripped the breath inside her. In her mind she saw a curling grey tower rising to meet the clouds, and her heart was jumping.

"Do you hear it?" cried Claudia. "What do you hear?"

"I do not know, madam. I am not sure."

"What do you hear, Aifa?" she demanded. "Girl! You hear something. Tell me!"

Aifa hesitated a moment, the answers gathering in a crowd. But she did not know how to voice them. Armies. Battle. Fire. Death. Each and all of them, at once.

"I think Londinium is under attack," she said.

Claudia took in a short, shallow breath.

"Boudicca," she said. It was not a question.

"Flee!" came a yell on the wind as Didius returned, the drumbeat of racing hooves drowning the distant sounds of battle and fire.

Urgently he beat a hand on the side of the wagon, as if to shake his mother free of any doubt. He leaned in towards her, his face red with sweat. He was struggling to keep the horse under control.

"It's burning!" he cried. "The city is ablaze! Flee! Now!"

"But we must get help," shouted Septimus, reining in the other horses as they grew restless with fear. "We must find the master. The governor, the army…"

"They know," said Claudia, slowly, quietly.

"Know? Are you mad?" yelled Didius, and the mare reared back so straight that Aifa thought he would slide to the grass.

"The invitation," Claudia said. "Don't you see? It was your father's way of making sure we left without chaos. Without terror. It was a way of saving our lives."

"But why did the governor not return," cried Septimus, "to protect the city? He would not abandon the people! I cannot believe he would give up before he began!"

"It is not for us to question the orders of the governor!" cried Claudia, her voice straining with agitation. "No soldier can be in two places at once! He cannot quell rebellion in the west and defend Londinium at the same time!"

Didius beat his mount so hard that Aifa stared at the whip clenched in his hand – with a fierce will that it might be knocked to the ground should the mare decide she had had enough.

"We have been spared," said Claudia. "You have been spared. Be thankful."

Aifa could imagine the fear, the running and screaming, the helplessness she remembered so well. She could imagine Brigit, hear her voice, see the terror in her eyes. And Septimus must have been imagining too.

"With respect, I cannot, madam, give thanks when hundreds will die," he told her, the emotion breaking out of his clipped speech.

"Then you should learn gratitude!" snapped Claudia.

She was rigid, pale and hard. Aifa saw in her no compassion, no pity for the dying, no fear for her own husband. She cared only for survival. Thinking once more of her own mother, Aifa knew for sure that this regal woman could never care for her like the strong but tender woman she might never see again.

It was only then that they realised Didius was galloping away, back to the flames, turning a horse with no wish to obey.

"No!" protested Septimus. He might have gathered up the reins as if to take the wagon after him, but his mistress held out her hand.

"Let him go," she said. "He is many things, but not, at least, a coward. Let him give his father a reason to be proud of him."

Aifa stared. Her son would die. But if he could save one citizen of Londinium, perhaps he would cross the river to glory in their underworld. Perhaps she had been wrong to think she knew what only the gods could see – the heart she had thought he lacked.

And if he could save only one life, let it be Brigit!

But she knew that for Didius only Roman lives would be worth saving. None but the gods could protect Brigit. And where had they been, any of the gods, when her father had met the same kind of fate at the hands of choking smoke and hungry flame?

"Hurry!" cried Claudia. "Away!"

The three of them did not linger to listen to the sounds of the dying city. Septimus chivvied the horses into a gallop and drove the wagon to safety without a backward glance. Silent tears were filling Aifa's eyes as she looked away across the hills so that her mistress might not see them fall. As soon as she could, she faked sleep, and before long the rhythmic breathing next to her told her that Claudia had managed to forget everything that she could not.

They travelled on, far beyond the crackle of flame, but hours later, as twilight shrouded their path, the sky remained dark but livid over a scarlet and gold Londinium, glimpsed from the fresh air of high green land many miles beyond the fire.

Chapter Ten

Knucklebones

Arriving at the villa, which was as elegantly palatial as she had predicted, Claudia made herself at home. She drank too much wine. She ate until Aifa felt sure there would be vomit to wipe from the unfinished mosaic floor. And every night, while Aifa breathed feverishly through the same nightmares, her own village melting into Londinium, and Brigit into Acco, her mistress's sleep was sound.

In an adjoining room where she lay, on hand as always should her mistress need anything, Aifa was afraid to close her eyes. But even in her wakefulness the flames filled the darkness. Part of her, listening to the stillness of Claudia's peace, wanted to hear tears. It was not that she wished her pain. She could not wish that on anyone, not even Didius. But it would help her to understand the mother whose son had ridden off to die. Surely grief for the dead was a feeling they could share – for the countless victims of Boudicca's rage, Roman and British, slaves and masters.

Though the only sound she heard was the steady rhythm of tearless breathing from the huge, ornate bed across the half-patterned floor, Aifa had enough tears for both of them and cried them, as quietly as she could, through the nights that were the longest she'd known.

And the days were little better. Lazier, cleaner and less greasy than Londinium days, they nonetheless dragged on emptily. The Lady Flavia's own slaves kept the villa swept and warm, the household fed. She had little to do beyond styling Claudia's hair, polishing her jewellery and ensuring that her robes were taken to be washed in the steaming laundry. But Claudia rarely spoke to her, and the fondness Aifa had once imagined no longer softened her eyes.

The eyes of her sister Flavia were dark and stony as winter skies. While Aifa knew too well that Claudia could be sunny one day and cold the next, in Flavia the frost never melted. Since the fierce-looking beauty showed Claudia no sisterly affection that Aifa could see, she could hardly be expected to spare any kindness for the rest of the household. Aifa averted her eyes whenever she was around, and hoped she was not noticed.

Septimus asked his pupil, eventually, if she wished to resume her lessons. She was glad to do so, but more than poems and maps she wanted answers he could not give.

Was there news of Didius or the master? And in the house where she had lived, had any survived?

The Lady Flavia's husband, who had also been with the army in the hilly west, had not returned home, and no word had found its way out to the country. One or both sisters might now be a widow. Not that either showed any desire to mourn.

"Of this, though," Septimus told Aifa, "I am sure – the Emperor will order the rebuilding of Londinium, and it will be another Rome of glass and stone, marble and tile. It will be magnificent! And no savage queen will ever destroy it."

Aifa told him with the flatness of her silence that she did not care about stone or tile, magnificence or Rome. She only cared about the people.

"Jupiter saw fit to spare you," he told her. "You are blessed by the gods, Aifa."

For a moment Aifa imagined she felt Epona against her thigh. She would have liked to touch it gratefully. But the necklace was safe – and hidden as she herself would have liked to be.

"Perhaps," said Septimus, "you should go to thank Epona while we are here."

Aifa stared. What did he know of Epona? And where was here? What could he mean? She could not be sure whether he was mocking her. And she was troubled. Thankful though she was, what sense did it make that she had been chosen, if her family had all died before her?

"But why have I lived, when so many were not spared?"

"That is not for you to know."

"You blame Boudicca, but I blame the Emperor who ordered soldiers here in ships," Aifa told him, her voice quiet but thick with feeling. "If she is cruel, Roman soldiers made her so."

Of course she had overstepped the mark, and by a Roman mile. But he only looked away, and rose to turn his back on her.

"I have nothing to teach you after all," he said, and walked away. "You know everything already, it seems. So young and so sure…"

"No!" she protested. "I'm not…I'm not sure of anything! How can I be? I just try…to believe…"

He turned back, and clasped her hand in both of his.

"You are loyal to your country, your gods, your traditions. Just as I used to be. Just as I still am."

She nodded, and looked up at him with a warm smile of gratitude. This wise, freckled little man was in fact her only friend.

But the following morning, when she looked for him, he was nowhere to be found. The slaves she asked only told her he had gone.

Aifa hesitated to approach her mistress. Since they had arrived in this place, she had become more unpredictable than ever, and it seemed to Aifa that she was becoming as hard as her sister.

Later that day she was summoned unexpectedly to brush the Lady Claudia's hair, and found the two women together, the atmosphere between them icy. They took as little notice of each other as of the two girls who served them. Then as Aifa brushed her mistress's hair, Claudia suddenly sat upright and rose without a word or glance, gliding past Flavia and out of the room.

The lady of the house closed her eyes as if to enjoy the peace now that she was alone. Aifa, left with the brush in her hand, began to slip away in the hope that she would not be noticed.

The strident voice stopped her in her tracks.

"Where are you going?" she demanded.

"After my mistress," Aifa told her quietly.

"You remind me of a dog that keeps hanging around for the next kicking," Flavia drawled.

Though her eyes had closed again, Aifa did not dare shape the face she would have liked to pull.

"If you have been looking for that foolish old tutor, you need not waste your time," she heard as she withdrew. "We have no need of him here," added Flavia, "any more than we have need of you."

Then set me free, thought Aifa. But only her eyes dared to say it. She nodded silently, and slipped away as the sharp voice called after her.

"My sister is...delicate. Vulnerable. She believes what she wants to believe. But I assure you, little girl, that you will find me a very different proposition."

As Aifa settled down that night she wondered whether she had been safer in Londinium, with the bullying boy, than with these sisters who could not agree about who she was.

Chapter Eleven

Accused

Aifa did not sleep well. When she woke the following morning, there was Claudia, standing over her, watching. Startled, she sat up nervously, eyes wide with alarm.

"Still you are afraid of me! Why, when I have treated you with nothing but kindness? Can you not see how much…how I long for you to trust me?"

Aifa was dumb.

"You are so like her," she said softly, walking to the window and looking out across the hills. "My little Livia. I see her every time I look in your eyes. So fair, and so pretty."

What could Aifa say? She only hoped there would be no more drunken confusion and no more invitations to worship gods that meant nothing to her.

"Juno is the goddess of women, of childbirth and motherhood," Claudia explained. "I can only believe that she took pity on me, and sent you to console me."

"Mistress," said Aifa, gently, but with conviction, "I have a mother."

Claudia looked back at her, the morning light across her pale face.

"I do not ask you to love me. I do not know if I have any love left to give you. But I ask you...I command you to allow me this. Be like a daughter to me. Let me comb your hair, like a mother would. Let me sing to you, and tell you stories. And when the building is complete, of the shrine to all-generous Juno, bow down with me, and thank her for bringing you to me."

Though she begged, Aifa sensed an order in disguise. Claudia was mistress here, not mother, and she expected to be obeyed. Startled still, Aifa was touched by pity, but it was fear that held her silent.

"What have you to say?" prodded Claudia.

She returned to Aifa's bed and reached out to take her hand, but Aifa rose and bowed her head, choosing humility. She hoped it would be enough.

"Speak, child. What have you to say to me?"

Still Aifa looked down at her feet, and mumbled, "Nothing, mistress. Slaves have nothing to say."

For a moment there was anger in those outlined eyes, but it melted away as she looked in Aifa's own.

"You will see. You will be glad. We will comfort one another in our loneliness."

"I am sorry for your loneliness," she whispered truthfully.

Perhaps it was the wrong reply. Perhaps this grand and powerful woman did not need her pity. Or perhaps it moved her more than she wanted her to see. Claudia swept away, slowly, almost silently, her head as high and her back as straight as ever.

With no duties to perform, Aifa spent much of the day in a tree, thinking. As she watched, she breathed in the scents of the garden and felt the breeze in her hair. She was swinging a leg, humming a tune her mother sang and remembering freedom, when she was summoned to attend to the sisters.

They seemed tense as they waited for guests to arrive. Aifa thought at first that the atmosphere stemmed from anxiety. Perhaps they believed these visitors would bring news of the survival of their husbands. Or their death.

But soon she realised that in fact the air between the sisters was thick with hostility. All the slaves grimaced discreetly at their raised voices carrying across the courtyard, and some of them thought that the small pot smashed to smithereens in the course of one such disagreement was no accident. Aifa could not help wondering, in view of the way Flavia looked down her long nose at her, whether their arguments had something to do with her.

It made her so nervous that the following morning she let a comb slip from her hand. She let out a little gasp the moment it caught Claudia's cheek. Her mistress flinched, gave her a quick reproachful glare, but said nothing. Then minutes later Aifa dropped a brooch, and though it was undamaged, Flavia snapped sharply at her.

"Clumsy little barbarian!" she cried.

Claudia scowled at her.

"I would ask you to leave her alone."

"Go," Flavia told Aifa. "Your mistress is unwell."

She looked at Claudia, who had covered her face with her hand.

"It's true," she said. "I am sick…at heart."

"Can I fetch you something, mistress?" Aifa asked her. "Wine, perhaps?"

"Are you deaf, girl? I told you to leave us!" roared the deeper, more piercing voice.

"Aifa, stay…"

Claudia reached out, but Aifa did not wait to be shouted at twice.

She returned instead to the shelter of the tree, picked an apple from its branches and ate it slowly, savouring its flavour. It was safer here, and easier to breathe.

If she could have closed her eyes to absorb the sunlight and fragrance, if she could have put aside all the petty cruelties and persistent fear, the misery might have left her for just a few moments in the warm breeze. If only she could have thought of her family without the stabbing pain that always filled the peace.

But she had barely finished the apple when cries broke out below her and she heard her name. Descending to the bottom branch, she saw Flavia's favourite slave marching towards her, her mouth set in a purposeful line.

"Down!"

She waited, wondering for a moment what would happen if she stayed in the branches. But picturing the hunting dogs that would be gathered to snap at her ankles with slavering jaws, she jumped down. The woman grabbed her by the wrist.

"You're hurting me!" she protested, but the grip was tight.

A girl slave hurried across to hold her other arm, and they dragged her across the gardens, back to her sleeping quarters, all the while spitting out the names of animals of which she reminded them.

There she saw her bedding disturbed, and a large gold ring lying in the midst of the disarray.

"All that special favour and you are nothing but a thief!" cried the older woman, who dressed Flavia and was always at her side.

"No..." she began, "I am not..." but she stopped, hardened the tears that might have wobbled her voice, and lifted her head, silent but proud.

One minute these people bought and sold her like a chest. The next they doted on her like a pet. Then she was a gift from the gods, a surrogate daughter, and now a thief. And none of it changed who she was or what she would always be. She need not defend herself to them. And she must not beg for mercy.

"You are to be beaten."

The announcement from the girl, who seemed to take pleasure in it, was unnecessary. Aifa knew what happened to anyone who stole so much as a loaf of bread, let alone a ring of gold. She had learned soon enough that Roman punishments were based on shame, and acute pain.

Instantly Aifa saw that someone wanted her to suffer for something she had not done. Was it this favourite of Flavia's, aiming to please her mistress? Or could she simply be following orders from the lady of the house herself? Did Flavia hate her so much?

Two slaves grabbed her then, one on each side holding her with jealous force, making her kneel on the cold tiled floor. Clenching her fists tightly, she dug her nails into her palms as she waited. The first lash of the whip came at last against her back, vicious in its bite. The second followed, then the third, tearing into ripped flesh, pulling it open like lips parting wider and wider as the agony increased. She had never known such relentless pain. Aifa closed her eyes, but the darkness was inside her. She was falling off her father's huge black horse, and fire was everywhere. Aifa fell into a kind of burning sleep in which there was no peace or rest.

When she woke, her back was hot as flame and stiff as a pillar. Her eyes were still half-closed as she drank the water offered by an unseen hand.

"Face down," said Claudia.

Her mistress did not lower herself to attend the wounds of a dirty slave, but she made sure that other hands bathed them, while she sat watching from across the room until she was satisfied. No one uttered a word – not Claudia, not the slaves who dabbed at the cut flesh without care or gentleness, and not Aifa, biting her lip to stop her cries in her throat.

She remembered the courage her father had taught her, and clung to the silence as if it were her life.

"I did not want to believe you stole from me," she heard, at last, Claudia's voice flat and cold. "But you have deceived me. My sister was right. I was deluded by grief. You are a barbarian, nothing more."

Though she wanted to protest her innocence, Aifa could not heave the words quickly enough into her dry mouth. And Claudia gave her little chance.

Face down on the floor, blood and water trickling down her back, Aifa heard her mistress walk away. There was anger inside her now, alongside the pain, and a kind of outrage. It was not so much the beating itself as the dishonour. Claudia should have known her better. She should have defended her against a sister for whom she had no love.

Now at last Aifa knew that she was nothing to her, less than nothing. She had taken away Claudia's hope, and theft like that could never be forgiven.

Chapter Twelve

Plan

It was several days before Aifa could resume her duties, and during those days she was left almost completely alone. Her only visitors were slaves who saw that she was fed – with small piles of stale leftovers. More precious was the sleep, and at least she was allowed plenty of that. She surrendered to it gladly, grateful to escape the sharp and sticky soreness of her back.

Of the two noble ladies who controlled her fate she saw and heard nothing. No messages of concern found their way from Claudia, no orders and no kindness from anyone at all, until she woke on the third morning to find a jar of soothing oil beside her.

Dazzled by the sunlight through the window, she asked the slave who arrived with food whether it had been her mistress who left the jar.

"How would I know? She's gone, anyway. They both have, my mistress and yours."

"Gone where?"

"They don't tell me!"

Perhaps in search of her master, or news of him? Aifa did not wish him dead. Her mistress had lost too much already. But she was not sorry for their departure. It was as if a noose around her neck had been untied.

Then, later, as she found she could reach and stretch without silent tears, she was sent for and told to report to the stables, to replace the boy who helped the groom. Since he was sick, someone must feed the remaining horses and clear away their mess. For Aifa, it was a pleasure. She walked slowly, glad to feel the light. For once, the sun was bright enough, the sky blue enough, even for those who mourned the loss of golden Rome. As she crossed the courtyard, smelt the horses and heard them whinny restlessly, she closed her eyes a moment to enjoy the warmth of the breeze.

The thought that entered her mind shocked her. So obvious, so simple! How ridiculous that it had never occurred to her before!

If she were to disappear while her mistress was away, who else would miss a small, pale slave who did not even belong? If she dared to steal a horse, she would of course be hunted down and punished without mercy, but on foot, slipping away unnoticed, who would care enough to mount a search?

The groom had his back to her. She had no reason to suppose she had been seen or heard. Aifa stopped, and turned back towards the house, but at the fountain ducked down and watched him grooming the white mare and whistling quietly. Wherever she looked, glancing around her in every direction, she saw only slaves, scrubbing, sweeping around the pool, working to build the shrine. No soldiers, no master, no guests. All she had to do was hold her nerve, find and trust Epona, and leave.

There was a basket a pace or two from the fountain, with fresh green pickings from the herb garden strewn across it. Aifa picked it up, and marched purposefully through the garden, reaching down to pick a few stems while she looked around her just to be sure. Then she carried it out, between the gooseberry bushes, pausing every now and then to pluck a few fruits and drop them in the basket.

Before she started to dig away the earth with a stone, she glanced back to the verandah and up to the bedrooms that overlooked the garden. Her necklace was there, just where she had buried it. Aifa rubbed earth from the copper, brushed it with her thumb, and wiped it on her rough brown tunic before she hung it round her neck, cold but reassuring against her skin. In spite of the racing heartbeat below, she felt strangely safe.

Only the wall remained, guarded at the entrance but little higher than a man – low enough for a girl who could mount her father's huge black stallion years before she could reach to stroke its muzzle.

She chose the stretch behind the tree where blossom grew thickest. The jump from the top of the wall was no more than a drop, eyes closed, down to welcome grass, and just a short sprint beyond, woodland lay waiting. Aifa ran, and didn't stop, until her heart was bursting in her chest and her cheeks hot and swollen with breathlessness. Only when a tangle of roots lay in dust at her feet, and the sunlight no longer reached her through the broken roof of leafy branches, did she buckle at the waist, the air hard in her lungs.

Gasping deep gulps of sweet air, she realised she was free.

Aifa had not been blessed with her mother's gift of reading the wind and the earth like a map. She had no precise idea where she was or how to find her way from there to anywhere else. She had no home. She could not be sure she had a family. But with a sudden rush of certainty she knew where she must go.

Chapter Thirteen

Bad Meat

The woods were a shield, but she had to work her way through them before they became a maze to trap her. When she ducked down under branches that blocked her way, the bending stretched the broken skin, opening the wounds so that they caught on the rough threads of her tunic. When she felt herself attacked from behind by branches that took her unawares, the sudden, beating heat smarted like a fever. Though it was cool in the woods, sweat trickled salty into the cuts, while her face and hands felt icy white.

At first, Aifa had drunk the scents of the bark, the earth, the greenness, with joyous relief. But now her step became less steady and the world around grew hazier. Her stomach ached with hunger, but the thirst hurt more. She had drunk nothing in the woods but the berry juice she had squeezed into her dry mouth and trickled down her bramble-scarred tunic.

She needed water.

At last the trees began to thin, revealing an undimmed brightness of sky. She was almost at the edge of the woods, and all she could see beyond was the glare of the sun. Breaking out of the shade of the remaining branches, she found that a mellow glow had softened the afternoon heat. Evening was on its way. Time, she told herself, moved faster than she could, and darkness would follow. She must be ready for it. Aifa sat down, at the edge of the wood and looked around her, using her nose and her ears as well as her eyes.

She must eat and drink, she must sleep, and above all she must keep herself safe. Faith in Epona was one thing; she had to use her wits as well as her heart. Since landing the other side of the wall she had avoided people, but now she was not sure she had the strength to survive alone. Looking across the hills, she saw no sign of settlement. No homes meant no supper, and no shelter for the night. She would have been glad of company. But Aifa was no longer a trusting child.

Before she saw him, she smelt him, and a trace of smoke and steaming food on the breeze. But she heard him first, or the snap of the branches as he broke through them and out of the woods, not far from where she had emerged herself only minutes before.

The boy carrying wood, a huge armload of wood, did not look surprised, or even very interested, to see her. But in his glance she saw no aggression, no suspicion. Nothing, she thought, to fear. For a long moment they stared at each other in silence.

"Help me carry this," he said, "and there's stew on the fire."

She stretched out both arms and let him offload a bundle of branches. In spite of the back that stiffened to support the weight, she made sure she did not wince.

"You ill?" he asked, taking in the pallor of her face, the cold sweat on her forehead and chin.

"Just sore," she said, and he leaned round to see the old blood caked on the tunic, the fresh blood soaking in.

"Who beat you?" he asked, but though she thought there was kindness in his voice, she did not choose to tell him.

Careful not to lag behind, she followed him, further than she hoped, to the nearest roundhouse in a small settlement. Her heartbeat quickened as he called out a greeting and a woman emerged from inside.

"Put it on the fire," she said, nodding towards a flagging pile of ash below an untended pot. "You've been too long. It's almost out."

"Can she eat?" he asked, nodding back towards her. "She's hungry."

His mother scrutinised her a moment before deciding.

"You don't look like you eat too much."

"I don't. Thank you."

The woman's eyes were on the horse around her neck. Aifa's fingers rushed to guard it. She had not endured Roman slavery to lose her only possession to a countrywoman's greed or fancy.

Without waiting for permission, the woman reached for it. As the hand met hers, Aifa made the decision to drop her guard, and let her fingers fall. The woman held it a moment, examined it closely and looked her in the eyes.

89

Aifa had an uncanny feeling that her mind was being read.

"It's not far," she said. "You're close. Another day's walking, if you're strong."

Aifa smiled. Who should she trust, if not a follower of Epona?

"She's not. She's hurt," interjected the boy.

"I'm strong," said Aifa, giving him a reproachful glance.

His mother looked her over, and drew breath at the sight of her back. Her touch was gentle.

"Eat first," she said.

Aifa could so easily have slept. But while she waited for the flames to flare into enough life to cook the stew, she kept her hand on the necklace and her eyes wide open. They watched her, but though she felt their curiosity, mother and son did not pester her with questions.

She ate her fill, and afterwards she let the woman tend her cuts, washing them first and then gently smoothing in a thick and pungent ointment green with leaves and herbs. Her tunic was taken, damped down and draped to dry near the fire while she wrapped herself in a rough cloak lent by a neighbour.

As darkness fell and the mother brought a skin to still her shivering, Aifa allowed the warmth of the food inside her, and the flames that reddened her face, to lull her into sleep.

Dimly, as she drifted, she heard mother and son speculate about her, mock her quiet fierceness, commend her bravery, and wish her well. But she was too sleepy to reply. Horses raced, hooves beating, through her dreams.

Chapter Fourteen

Horses

When Aifa awoke they had gone, leaving her water, and bread wrapped in a worn rag. The pain no longer raged in her back, but as she stood she did not feel the strength she had boasted.

The sun told her it was late morning. Feeling fresher and more hopeful, she splashed a little of the water in her face and took a bite of the bread. There was no sign of the boy or his mother, but looking around her uncertainly she saw that in the dust at her feet was scratched a map.

It wasn't much. But perhaps it would be enough. The kindness made her smile, but she was sorry that she could see no one to thank. Smoke trailed weakly up from the fire that had been left to die. Through its smell she caught the aroma of last night's stew, stirring inside her a faint nausea, but she could hear nothing, no voices, no sawing of wood or beating of iron. The thick, dusty stillness of the sun-dried village began to seem unsettling as she watched the other huts for a sign of life. Wondering whether old women or babies slept inside, she wished they would wake. Or snore, or cry.

Dismissing her growing fear, Aifa breathed deeply and looked down once more at the scratch marks in the dust that pointed her where she must go. She could do it. She needed no one but Epona to guide her. But all through her many months of captivity she had survived alone, with friendship no more than a glimmer in twilight. He was just a boy, no less strange to her than Didius, but he might have cared, just a little, given time. She would have liked, at least, to say goodbye. Now she would never even know his name.

She felt sure before she peered into his home that it was empty, and was about to walk on across their fields of ripening corn when something on the ground caught her eye. It looked at first like a small heap of autumn leaves, brown and red, piled damp and bedraggled in the dirt. But as she drew closer she saw the sightless eye gleam, the beak open as if about to squawk, and the bones, peeled of flesh, angling out of the puddle of blood-splashed feathers. Aifa had fed and eaten many chickens, but this was not the work of human beings.

She looked back to the roundhouse and across the fields to the neighbouring homes, where smoke still drifted faintly through the walls up into the bright sky. The sound that made her catch her breath was like a yawn, but deep and rasping. Beneath it lay the slow rhythm of a padded tread that came to a sudden stop.

Aifa turned to see a massive wall of dark brown fur rise up on thick back legs to let loose a sound not unlike thunder. She had never seen such an animal before, not in the towering, growling, fur-coated flesh. But she had seen its picture, and thanks to Septimus, knew its Latin name. Ursus. She was looking at a bear, and incredulous terror held her rooted, too heavy to move and almost too frightened to breathe.

Its two front paws fell soft but heavy to the ground, and it waited, still, as it held her in its gaze. Her paralysed brain stirred, suddenly, frantically. Should she move? Could she move? Where could she go, and would it let her? Its belly swung like a giant sack, and its tongue hung out between teeth she barely glimpsed, but imagined all too clearly. There was no need to wonder whether it was hungry. One cockerel would satisfy neither its appetite nor its lust for blood, but one girl, however scrawny, just might.

No one had told her not to run. It was her heart and leaden feet that told her that. Instead she began to walk very slowly backwards, her eye on the bear's eye, towards the roundhouse where weapons might lie. A spear, perhaps. A spear would do, if she had the strength to lift it and the skill to hit her target! As she backed away, the bear moved just a little, its shoulders rising like hills of fur before falling again. It followed very slowly after her, lumbering along on all fours, in no great hurry yet covering more ground with one step than she could in three.

Though its open mouth gaped like a dark red cave, the sudden roar was not deep enough to have broken from that great throat. Instead it came out of the field. There corn was beaten down by the familiar figure of a running, shouting boy waving his fist in the air. It was the boy who had offered her hospitality, the boy with no name. He had not abandoned her to a gory death after all. But a rasping growl answered him as the creature reared up again, its yellow teeth bared in a snarl.

Out of the corner of her eye Aifa saw the fire, and the branch lying beside it. Grabbing it, she dug it deep into the heart of the smoke, where the little glow of red had not yet cooled to useless ash. She stirred it around and out again, the tip of it flickering into the slowest, tiniest flame. The bear, caught between the roaring boy advancing and the brightness of the stick she was brandishing, slumped down. Into a run it lumbered, powering away to the trees.

Arrows flew after it as the boy stopped to fire his bow. One hit its rump, piercing the skin beneath the fur, clinging at an angle as it stumbled, but only for a moment. They stood without speaking, watching the thick back legs beating through the undergrowth, barely faltering, until all fell still. Only the strange, foreign smell remained in the warm air.

Then the boy threw a pile of wood onto the fire, and stoked it into life, glancing from flames to trees and back again, without speaking. She knew he was still afraid because she was afraid too. But no sound came from the wood and as the fire began to blaze he sat down, his bow beside him.

"What was it?" he breathed, and allowed himself a nervous grin.

"Have you never seen a bear before?"

He shrugged.

"I'm going to hunt him down. Then we'll bake his flesh on the fire and he'll feed the village for a week. I'd like to see his ugly head on a post."

Aifa let him see she was less impressed by him than by the bear.

"It's a magnificent head. He'll want to keep it. And I doubt whether he thinks a lot of yours."

He gave her a doubtful look, as if he didn't know whether to grin again or scowl at her rudeness.

"The Romans train men to fight animals like that. I'm strong and I'm fit. Maybe they'd train me one day."

She could not believe her ears.

"You'd join the Roman army?"

"Perhaps. Don't you admire them? Have you seen their weapons? They're unbeatable."

"Unbeatable! Have you not heard of Boudicca?" she cried, suddenly prouder of the Iceni queen than she had ever felt before.

"She's dead! They say she killed herself rather than be taken to Rome. She caught them by surprise, that's all, but it couldn't last. She was bound to be defeated in the end."

Aifa took a moment to consider the news. It was hard to know how to feel about Boudicca, but she knew how she felt about the army that had finally conquered her.

"These soldiers you want to join are the invaders who came to attack us, to murder our fathers. They are not our friends."

Aifa's voice had wavered, but who was she to talk, she who had served them, obeyed their orders, eaten their scraps?

"I want to be a gladiator," he said, "or race chariots. When I'm older."

"Why?" Aifa stared, unable to understand this boy. "People die for sport. Why would you want to die?"

"If I was frightened of dying I wouldn't have saved your life!"

"I saved myself," she protested.

"I needn't have bothered to come running, then!"

"We both …saved my life."

"If you like."

She threw another log on the fire.

"I don't know your name," she said.

"My name is Cathbad," he said, and almost smiled.

"I'm Aifa," she told him.

"I thought you'd scream and run. That thing would have killed you then."

He sounded so matter of fact about it that she tried not to look as frightened as the thought made her, now that she had time to think about what might have been.

"It didn't kill anyone, did it?" she asked him suddenly, remembering the chicken. "Your mother! Is your mother safe?"

He nodded towards the fields.

"She's working."

"I don't know," Aifa said, choking suddenly, "if I have a mother."

He made no reply.

"Why did everyone go and leave me?"

It sounded more pitiful than she meant it to, and the crack in her voice had not yet healed.

"We didn't all run away and abandon you, if that's what you think," he grinned. "Did you think we kindly left your bear its breakfast?"

She felt silly and a little ashamed.

"No. Of course not."

"Not much of a breakfast. You wouldn't fill him up, a brute like that. You wouldn't fill a chicken."

He laughed at his own joke, and it was a while before he saw that she was not joining in.

"We let you sleep, that's all. You needed days of it. You look like you could do with a lot more."

"I'm not tired," lied Aifa, lifting her shoulders and trying not to show it when her back burned with the stretching.

They had cared about her after all. But it made no difference, she told herself. She belonged nowhere. Not in Londinium, or the country house, and not here with these strangers who were like her and yet so different.

"I'm going now," Cathbad announced, looking back to the fields where Aifa could make out the shape of his mother. "Be safe, Aifa."

"I will."

He grinned.

"Don't fight any more bears."

"I'll try not to."

As he headed away, and she looked once more at the markings in the dirt, just for reassurance, she called after him.

"Are you sick, Cathbad?"

He turned and grimaced.

"My mother did not mean to give you bad meat. I ate it too. I've thrown it up already. I'll live."

He walked on and turned to call, "You too, I hope, if your goddess wills it. Thanks to me."

Aifa could not be sure how much the cramps in her stomach sprang from the stew and how much from terror. She felt suddenly as if she might be sick too. Realising that she did not want the boy to go, she wished she had an excuse to call him back, but he was running, shrinking into the distance, without so much as a backward glance or farewell wave. Like poor Brigit, he was not to be her friend.

Aifa had been alone for so long that she wondered whether she would ever again exchange real smiles or share the feelings she was used to concealing. But she lived. Epona would not allow her to weaken. Trying to banish the bear from her mind, Aifa set her thoughts instead on a great white horse.

Chapter Fifteen

Journey

At first, as Aifa wandered, faltering and sore, she refused herself the luxury of rest. Instead she pushed herself on, ruthlessly ignoring the weakness in her legs and the waves beating in her head. But her progress slowed as the landscape shifted around her. The heat and ice burned equally fiercely inside her skin, until she had no choice but to stop. More than once she slept, in the shelter of a tree, behind rocks, or simply on the grass where she slumped and did not move.

For much of the day she saw no one. She picked apples and berries, but could not stomach them. Her mouth was acid with the vomit, and so dry she felt her tongue would crack. By the time she detected the sound and scent of water, she had no strength left to run to it as she longed to do, to throw herself into it, to let it flow over her and into her. Though the rush of the river sounded like a roaring flood in her ears, the light on the water made it swirl in front of her, and as she drew nearer she reached out like a blind man to feel it run over her hands.

She had no hope of hearing the footsteps with so much sound echoing in her head. Perhaps if her desire for the pure, cool water had been less desperate, she would have sensed them, those other hands, large and dirty. They were tugging at the cord that hung the copper horse around her neck before she could smell them, smell the man crouched behind her, thick arms crushing her. She never saw his face. In the shadowy broken reflection below her, all she glimpsed was wavering blackness.

The next thing she knew, she was face down on the bank of the river, wet and muddy, gasping for breath. Somewhere in her head she could hear the sound of running. He had gone, and so had her mother's gift. For the first time since she left the country house, Aifa cried. She sobbed until her body shook.

Through all the months of her loneliness, Epona had been safe, a presence in a crack in a wall or warm under soft soil. She had known where to find and touch the symbol she trusted. It helped her remember the hands of the mother who had hung it around her neck. No Roman army, bully boy or hateful woman had succeeded in parting her from it. It had been hers, and all she had. Until now.

Aifa splashed water on her face, and let the air coldly lick it dry. Her skin felt tight as her heart.

But she was near. She must be near. Back came the certainty, uncrushable. She held up her head, stooped to cup water in her hands and let it stroke its way down her throat. Standing, her back stinging livid at the movement, she had to bend again to squeeze the water from the hem of her tunic. She brushed the straggly, damp hair from her eyes and cheeks. Aifa was sure she was much too close to give up now. Epona was still there with her. It was a faith that no one could take away.

The sun was low now in a creamy sky. On she walked, compelled by a force she did not understand and could not resist. The map in the dust had been lodged in the mist and spray of the storm in her brain, but it had led her here. And here she knew, within her reach, and in these hills, the place must be.

The last of the bread eaten, and her stomach swollen with stabbing pains, she wrapped the cloak tighter around her, the breeze flapping it against her bare legs. Above her, the clouds that had scudded softly, as slow as her struggle, began to race. Around her the wild wind gathered, like a new enemy, to attack.

Her mother had said that apart from the gods, the birds saw it best. And having no wings, Aifa felt at first almost blind. It was only the whiteness that guided her. Like a Roman placing stone in a mosaic she gathered in her imagination the pieces around her and tried to make of them a picture. Some of the dips and rims were so uneven that in her weakness she stumbled into them. Huge and mysterious, slicing through the grass and smoothed into pockets and curves, the whiteness of the chalk was so bright she could not fail to recognise it, eye by eye, limb by limb. Aifa's heart felt hot, held firm, forgetful of how to beat.

Afraid to tread in clumsy ignorance on any ear or hoof of it, on any part of this wall-less temple of the earth and air, she stepped back, and looked around her. She beat away the hair and the faintness, searching for a place that would offer wingless mortals the view they came to find. And wondering whether her mother had ever come to find it – or seen it whole, galloping free, only in death?

But the wind, growing stronger by the minute, seemed to drain the strength from her legs and she crumpled to the grass, her stomach heaving, her face taut and white.

The last she saw was a whirl of chalk and grass swirling faster than the sky, then darkness swallowing sun, wind – and sudden vomit – into silence. As it closed around her, Aifa glimpsed the death, sudden and irresistible, that had claimed her father. And as she glimpsed it, felt it gather, she found she had no strength to fight it. She had escaped fire, battle and slavery to fall victim to bad meat. And now she was flying over a vast white horse as it galloped silently through the night sky within her.

Through the darkness a warrior was carried high and lowered deep. Fire crackled. A whip lashed without mercy. Back in the grave, the mighty sword was laid on top of him, and the huge black beast lay down, meek and accepting, beside him. His people spoke of his courage and his strength. But gathered around to honour him, they melted, flesh into flame, flickering, beating like a whip. And hidden, but rising up from the roar, were screams. Her screams.

Brigit was not crying. She was scarred by burns, but her face was smiling as she reached out to Aifa. Their hands were close, but did not meet. And the slave girl slipped away from her, back into the darkness, out of reach, into the silence left by the dying fire and the fading screams. All around Aifa the blackness drifted like the unbroken cloud of an angry storm.

Another hand, white and jewelled, reached out for hers, drew close, fingertips shaped and smooth. But it was snatched away into a softness of tears.

At first, when the darkness cracked open to let in shards of light, Aifa's belief in her own death remained unshaken. The blackness had been so deep, and thick as hillside snow. But the gold through the crack was too bright for her eyes to deny it.

The voices, muffled and blurred, seemed to come from inside her head, and she felt blanketed in a fleece of sunlight, her own name floating softer than cloud. For the first time, Aifa knew she was not afraid of dying. The peace was warm and safe, and gently it surrounded her. But someone was holding on, refusing to let her float away on it. Someone was willing her to live.

The first reality she knew for sure was a hot tightness around her thumb, and a gurgle of laughter. The small face that stared into hers was faintly familiar, but the gripping finger had never held her so tightly.

"Sparrow?"

"Aifa!"

Her brother had learned to say her name.

"I knew," said another voice, the voice she'd missed most. "I knew you would find us. I believed... if we came here, if we waited long enough, there was a chance you'd come..."

As her mother's fingers stroked her forehead, Aifa felt the strength of their kindness so powerfully that tears thickened in her throat and silenced the reply she wanted to shape. Yet still no words would come but one.

"Epona..." she murmured.

Her mother nodded, and kissed her neck where Aifa's necklace had hung.

"For days, days too many to count, we have climbed the hill to look for you. The people nearby, who have sheltered us, begged me to rest. Give up. Wait to meet you in the otherworld. I could not wait," she smiled. "She led you here, to us."

105

Aifa sat up, reached out both arms and fell into the familiar warmth, the smell she'd known so well, the pattern of the rough, earth-stained tunic. It seemed so long, long ago that she had watched her mother weave the cloth while she crawled contentedly around the loom, playing with whatever she could grab, knowing nothing of freedom, occupying armies, or cities on fire. It was the cloth she'd pictured when she'd drawn her mother's smile in dreams.

"Are we safe now?"

"Safe now," echoed Sparrow, stretching short arms around her neck.

"And father?"

Her mother nodded.

"Safe too. We buried him, like a king. Have no fears for him."

Close by, a great black stallion snorted and stamped impatiently, too full of spirit for any grave.

"Ri saved us. He carried us away. Your father would have been very proud."

"Proud," said Acco, touching her nose before laying a grubby hand on her cooling cheeks.

Aifa was crying, but these were different tears, breaking from a better place, a place she thought she'd never find again.

So this was it. Here where the great white horse leapt across the hills, she had brought no sacrifice to offer, but the grace of the gods had granted what she longed for most. She knew it now for what it was, and she was thankful. She did not know how long she could hold on to it, but she would not forget it.

This was happiness.

Chapter Sixteen

End

When Aifa was strong enough they began the journey home. The village where her father had died was still scarred with the blackness of ash, not yet healed or concealed by nature's newborn green. But a mile away, close enough to remember, roundhouses had been built by the survivors. While she had lived in a different world, here the old life had begun once again without her.

There was so much to tell her mother that Aifa did not know where to begin. Her mother did not press her, but waited patiently for her to be ready. In spite of the joy that filled her daylight silences, Aifa's nights were cold and damp with nightmares.

In her sleep the fires still blazed. The flame was just as hungry and the eyes just as dark with fear. She pictured the inferno she had never seen up close, as Londinium burned and Boudicca roared tall in her chariot.

She heard the deep and angry battle cry, urging her to rise up and fight. She saw Flavia place a ring on dishevelled bedclothes, turn round and smile. She saw Claudia crying, looking for her, alone. And one night she saw Livia, the child her mistress had wanted her to be, lying in her coffin with her own eyes closed. Reaching out to touch the chill white skin, she felt the death in her own flesh and looked down on her own still, silent mouth.

But by day Acco led her out of all the dark memories into sunlight and play, noise and excitement. Aifa supposed that all the tragedy had passed him by while he was too young to make sense of it. His arms would not yet reach around her waist, but they joined round her neck when she lifted him. And he was more curious than ever, reaching out to touch everything that moved.

After several days of healing sleep her mother took Aifa to see the spot where her father was buried. Neither mother nor daughter spoke a word. Instead they stood still and silent in a ferocious wind, looking straight ahead at the clouds passing over the hills, never glancing down or picturing what the earth hid. She shed no tears and said no prayers. But Aifa was glad to be there, her family beside her. And her mother knew her ways, and let her be.

It was a long time before Aifa spoke of Septimus or the education he had given her, or of everything Claudia had taught her. She felt strange about her Roman learning. Still she was troubled by a clinging touch of guilt, as if she had betrayed her people and become some kind of traitor. There were little skills she could show her mother without such shame, but as for the knowledge of words, ideas and maps, and living creatures never seen in her world, she kept it secretly locked away. She knew her mother would not resent or blame her. But she did not know how to own it or what to do with it.

The world she had begun to glimpse was so much bigger, more frightening and more wonderful than she had dreamed before. She had seen and heard things that the other Silures could not imagine, things that had changed the way she looked at the old life into which she had been welcomed back. But when she was asked about the cruelty of the Romans, or their cleverness, she would only say, simply, that they were people, strange and different but also oddly the same.

Aifa could not know if there were battles ahead. Perhaps all over the land wilder fires would blaze to make way for small Romes. Perhaps the old ways of the tribes would be swallowed up into the rules of the Empire. It was hard to imagine resistance driving such an army back across the sea.

But if she were a queen like Boudicca, or a Druid with the ear of her people, what speech would she make? What orders would she give? How could she crave more blood and fire, more death and grieving? She was her father's daughter, but a different spirit sparked inside her. When she looked around her in the quietness of twilight, it was peace she felt. Not anger. Not hatred or bitterness.

Some things had not changed. The bulls still felt the need to charge. The robins were nesting again, and the males defended their territory with as much dark-eyed aggression as ever. And ahead of her were more ordinary days, filled with the same tedious hardship as well as sun. But they were days she would not live alone, or in fear. She was free and she was loved. In her head, as she watched and listened, thought and remembered, swinging her legs high in a tree, or lying awake by moonlight, were questions she would learn to answer. And when she found the truth, she would serve it. She would share it and walk by the light of it, for as long as the gods granted her breath to live.